FUTURE PERFECT

Suzanne Brockmann

A KISMET® Romance

METEOR PUBLISHING CORPORATION
Bensalem, Pennsylvania

To my faithful first draft readers Lee Brockmann, championship mom, and Deede Bergeron, most excellent friend.

And, of course, to Ed.

SUZANNE BROCKMANN

Suzanne Brockmann wrote her first romance novel in a spiral notebook with a pencil during Mr. Tucker's high school chemistry class. In the decade and a half since then, she has fronted an original Boston rock band, formed and conducted an a capella chorus called "Serious Fun," taught aerobic dance, gotten married to a cool guy and had two very cool children—Melanie and Jason. Throughout it all, she has been writing incessantly, although the pencil and notebook have long since given way to a personal computer. She finds it much easier to write without pretending to take chemistry notes and without Mr. Tucker talking in the background.

ONE

The early morning air was biting, and the ground was white with frost. But Juliana Anderson opened the kitchen door and stood at the screen, welcoming the cold. She closed her eyes for a moment, feeling the chill air sweep over her flushed face, feeling the perspiration on her forehead grow icy.

The smell of the pancakes cooking on the huge old griddle made her turn back to the work at hand.

It was breakfast time at 31 Farmer's Hill Road, the most illustrious bed and breakfast in all of Benton, Massachusetts.

The *only* bed and breakfast in all of Benton, thought Juliana wryly as she plucked the sticky buns from the hot depths of the ancient oven with one mittened hand even as she flipped the pancakes with the other.

She smoothed her apron, tucking away a stray wisp of her willful red-gold curls before hoisting up the heavy platter of warm buns and a pitcher of foaming milk. She opened the swinging door into the dining room with her back, smiling gently, always the gracious Victorian hostess, as she placed the food on the huge oak table.

Five of last night's six guests were already at the table. With any luck, the sixth would arrive shortly, and Saturday's breakfast would soon be history.

She smiled to herself at the expression. Life at 31 Farmer's Hill Road tended to be mostly history all of the time.

Juliana and her aunt Alicia ran the huge old Victorian house as if it were a guest house of the early 1900s, even to the point of dressing in period outfits when guests were in residence.

This morning, Juliana wore a stiffly starched white blouse with a high, standing collar and leg-of-mutton sleeves that were puffy at the shoulder but formfitting from the forearm to the wrist. The blouse was carefully tucked into a pale-gray, high-waisted, full skirt that trailed behind her as she walked.

"Will you be joining us this morning, Miss Anderson?" one of the guests asked as Juliana picked the large glass bowl of fresh fruit salad off the table.

"Of course, Mr. Edgewood." Juliana smiled. "After one more trip into the kitchen, I think."

Many of her guests stayed with her regularly as they traveled the Massachusetts Turnpike from Boston to points west. The Edgewoods had relatives in Ohio and booked a room whenever they passed through. She could count on seeing them at least four times a year. It was like a visit from friends. In fact, the Edgewoods had been among her very first customers when the bed and breakfast had opened nearly five years ago.

She enjoyed their company and looked forward to seeing them.

But not all her guests were like the Edgewoods.

Juliana piled the pancakes onto a plate and put them into the oven, pouring more circles of batter onto the griddle.

Some of her guests came and went without a word, without even a greeting. She shrugged. *Products of modern times*, she thought. *Most people have forgotten how to be friendly these days. Or even polite.*

She crossed to the old-fashioned, rounded refrigerator, pulling a huge plastic container of cut fresh fruit from its chilly interior.

Take, for example, last night's mystery guest, one Webster Donovan. Mr. Donovan had been due to arrive yesterday evening. Juliana had waited up 'til long past midnight, but the man didn't even bother to telephone. Bad manners. Very bad manners.

Filling the ornate glass fruit bowl, she covered the plastic container and put it back in the fridge.

Yet Mr. Donovan had booked a room for six consecutive weeks, she mused as she crossed to the stove and turned the pancakes. He was bound to turn up sooner or later. He was a writer—that much Alicia had told her after he'd called to make his reservation. Juliana had been hoping he was a little elderly man, someone friendly, someone who could entertain her with the stories of his life during the next six weeks of breakfasts.

Please, she thought with a flash of desperation, *let me like him. Don't make me have to endure a silent, surly, unpleasant, modern guest.* But if his failure to call last night was any indication of his manners, she was in for a long six weeks.

Juliana crossed back to the glass bowl, peeled several bananas, and quickly cut them into the already huge mound of fresh fruit. With a quick stir, she mixed the fruit, then went back to the stove for the pancakes.

Juliana picked up the plate heaped with steaming, aromatic pancakes and the huge bowl of fruit and backed toward the dining room door. But instead of the giving swing of the door, she slammed into something hard and unyielding.

No, some*one*, she thought in surprise, as a large hand, attached to a strong arm, encircled her waist to keep her from falling. Another hand snaked out and grabbed the plate of pancakes, leaving her to concentrate on the bowl of fruit, which, much to her relief, she didn't drop.

Sweet heavens, she breathed, closing her eyes in relief. That bowl was an antique, a work of art, valued at over five hundred dollars. Alicia had been suggesting for months now that they stop using it as common dishware, and it would have been too awful for Juliana to have to explain that she'd dropped it.

Juliana opened her eyes slowly, suddenly aware that whoever was holding her hadn't let go. In fact, he had put the plate of pancakes down on the sideboard and now wrapped his other arm around her.

She tried to pull free, but couldn't. She turned her head to find the roughness of a several-days-old growth of beard against her cheek. She took a deep breath, prepared to order him sharply to release her. But she was stopped by the most intoxicating mixture of male scents she'd ever come across.

He smelled like the outdoors, like the pine trees on the top of Sleeping Giant Mountain, like sun block, baby shampoo, and clean sweat. There was a touch of city about him, too. She could smell a trace of gasoline, or maybe it was oil, and an echo of stale cigarette smoke, as if he'd recently spent time with a heavy smoker. He didn't smoke himself. Juliana knew that without a doubt. His mouth was inches from hers and smelled only sweet. Like apple cider.

He must've stopped at Greene's Orchards just a few moments ago, Juliana thought, feeling oddly off balance.

Large fingers gently took the bowl from her hands, and still she couldn't find the words or the will to protest.

She turned her head to look up at him, and time seemed to stand still. It was only a few seconds, but it seemed like hours, days, centuries that she stood there, gazing into the bluest eyes she'd ever seen. They were an unreal shade of pure, deep crystal-blue, framed by sinfully long, dark lashes. Those eyes dominated his face. And his wasn't a face easily dominated. High cheekbones gave him an exotic cast. Thick, wavy black hair tumbled over a broad forehead. He had a straight nose, a strong chin, and a mouth . . . His lips were sensuous and beautifully shaped. Fascinated, she watched as he slowly moistened his lips with his tongue.

And still he held her tightly. She'd turned so that she faced him, and she could feel his thighs pressing against her. Long thighs, lean thighs . . . This man was tall. Juliana couldn't remember the last time she'd met a man that she couldn't stare down nose to nose. But judging from the crick in her neck, this man had to be at least six and a half feet tall.

His grip on her tightened, and she looked up into his eyes again. The sharp, crystal blue had somehow become softer, gentler, and she knew without a doubt that unless she moved quickly, he was going to kiss her.

She pulled away, eyes wide, feeling a flush creep into her cheeks.

"God almighty," he said, his voice a rich, husky baritone. "You're so beautiful."

She felt her color deepen. Unable to speak, she snatched the plate of pancakes and the bowl of fruit from the sideboard and disappeared into the dining room.

Catching a glimpse of herself in the gilt-framed mirror that hung on one wall of the dining room, Juliana was amazed at how calm and composed she appeared. Her face was slightly flushed, but the heat from cooking often did that. Redness in her cheeks didn't necessarily mean that a rough, handsome stranger had waltzed into her kitchen and grabbed her.

"More coffee?" she murmured, filling Mrs. Edgewood's cup with decaf.

How *dare* he come into her kitchen like that.

"Do sit down, dear," Mrs. Edgewood urged.

"One more trip to the kitchen," Juliana said, years of practice keeping her smile serene. "And this one will be the last. I promise."

She put the coffee pot back on the sideboard and pushed the kitchen door open. When the door swung shut behind her, her eyes were blazing.

The man was still standing in the same spot. He was wearing a worn pair of jeans, stained and grimy with grease—that was where the oil smell came from, Juliana realized. Over a dark T-shirt, he wore an unbuttoned plaid flannel shirt. The sleeves were rolled halfway up his forearms, and veins and tendons stood out against long, sinewy muscles. His hair was too short to pull back at the nape of his neck, but too long to be called short. It curled wildly about his head as if he hadn't bothered to comb it after waking up. And he looked as if he hadn't shaved in at least three days.

Yet somehow he managed to be the most attractive man she'd ever laid eyes on.

He looked back at her steadily, his deep-blue eyes still soft, his expression oddly uncertain.

Juliana felt another burst of anger—anger at herself for continuing to be attracted to this man. With very little difficulty, she managed to redirect her anger at him.

"Do you always manhandle unsuspecting women?" she asked, her voice low, but her tone unmistakably disapproving.

His expression shifted slightly. She saw disappointment flit across his face before his eyes seemed to harden, to crystallize. He smiled slightly, with just one corner of his mouth. "I 'manhandled' you so you wouldn't drop that beautiful glass bowl," he said, his controlled, accentless voice contradicting his roughshod appearance. "Why on earth are you using it for breakfast? It should be in a museum."

Was he an antique dealer? Juliana thought, then quickly rejected the idea. If he was, he would have dressed to the nines, not come here looking as if he'd spent the past few days working underneath a car. And he would have pretended the bowl was depression glass and tried to get it away from her for forty dollars or less.

"Are you Alicia?" he asked, his piercing gaze sweeping the length of her, missing no detail. It was all Juliana could do to keep from checking to see that her blouse was properly tucked in. "We spoke on the phone."

"No," she said, her tone matching his, just as polite. "I'm Miss Anderson, Miss Dupree's niece. You must be here to deliver the firewood. Please, just dump it next to the woodshed. Good day."

Juliana turned to go back through the swinging door, but he caught her arm. His large fingers seemed to burn her through the thin cotton of her blouse.

She looked at him in alarm. His smile was slightly mocking, as if he was well aware that his touch made her pulse quicken.

"I'm not here to deliver wood," he said. "I'm here to check in."

Juliana stared pointedly at his hand until he released her. She didn't allow her face to reveal the flurry of emotions passing through her. "Check-in's not until two o'clock, Mr. . . . ?" She let her voice trail off so he could fill in the missing name.

"Donovan," he said, and her heart sank down to her toes. "Webster Donovan."

Six weeks, Juliana thought desperately. Six weeks of being harassed, of having her clothing removed piece by piece by his eyes, the way he was doing right now.

"Do you always dress this way?" he asked.

"I could ask the same question of you," she replied tartly, chin up, meeting his exploring eyes almost defiantly.

He looked down at his grubby jeans, frowning slightly. "Oh yeah," he said, his voice apologetic. "Give me some time, and I assure you, I'll look better." He shot her a dangerous smile, an amused light in his eyes, and Juliana had to look away. He knew how good he looked, damn him, even splattered with grease the way he was.

"I was expecting you last night, Mr. Donovan," she said disapprovingly, trying hard to regain control over a conversation that was rapidly galloping away from her.

"I was expecting to *be* here last night," he said. "But I had car trouble. And, please, my friends call me Web."

"I see." Juliana pulled an extra place setting from the neatly stacked cabinets. "As long as you're here, Mr. Donovan—" she stressed the formal use of his full name "—why don't you join us for breakfast?"

"I had an Egg McMuffin in Stockbridge," Webster said.

"I can assure you," Juliana said, somewhat haughtily, "fast food can't be compared to the meals at this bed and breakfast."

He laughed. It was a low chuckle, a soft, sexy, lethal sound that made the hair on the back of her neck stand up. She kept her eyes carefully averted, not daring to look up into his handsome face.

"To tell you the truth," he said, "I'd much rather skip breakfast and get right to the bed part."

She did look at him then, more than slightly shocked. There was nothing in the tone of his voice that implied the double entendre, but his smile and his eyes were so unmistakably suggestive, his stance so masculine—

"Your room isn't ready," she said abruptly, putting the dishes on the counter with a clatter. "And I have to join my guests. Please feel free to use the sitting room or the front parlor until I've finished breakfast."

And with that, she turned on her heel and went out into the dining room.

Web stood staring, long after she had disappeared. He must be more tired than he'd thought. Why else would he be feeling so bothered by that encounter?

Yeah, okay, so she was beautiful. Big deal. He knew more than his share of beautiful women. But he closed his eyes, remembering the feel of her body against his.

For a moment, he'd actually believed that he'd finally met a woman he could fall in love with. For a moment, he'd actually believed that he could fall in love, that he'd even want to.

Hell, for an earth-shattering moment, he'd even believed in love at first sight.

He drew in a deep, shaky breath.

Shaky?

He frowned. He was exhausted, and the fatigue was really throwing him off center. No sir, love had nothing to do with— God, he didn't even know her first name! Miss Anderson, she'd called herself.

He pushed open the door to the dining room. His eyes found her instantly. She was sitting at the end of the table, at the far side of the room. She glanced up only briefly before she looked away, pink tingeing her fair complexion.

Web's chest tightened sharply just at the sight of her. He forced himself to turn away, to walk slowly out of the room. But he stopped at the doorway and looked back. She was watching him, her greenish eyes apprehensive.

The same tight sensation gripped him as their eyes

met again, and instantly he knew what was making him feel so odd. It was desire, lust, animal magnetism. He wanted her.

And he might not have believed in love at first sight, but he sure as hell believed in lust at first sight.

TWO

Juliana quickly put the milk and other perishables into the refrigerator and untied the apron from her slim waist before she went looking for Mr. Donovan.

The sitting room was empty, and the front entry hall held a large battered suitcase and three huge computer boxes, but no sign of Webster Donovan.

She opened the heavy front door and stepped out onto the wide, wraparound porch. The air was still chill enough for her breath to hang in front of her. No, he wasn't out here either.

Back inside the house, she started up the curving staircase, heading for the library. When Juliana had first started this business, the library had been her fifth guest bedroom. But she'd soon found that she didn't need the extra money once a dent had been made in the improvement loan payments. And the difference between having eight potential guests and ten was immense when it came to cooking and laundry. Besides, she needed a place to keep all Alicia's books.

Alicia was going to turn eighty in two more years, and Juliana was convinced that her great-aunt hadn't thrown a single book away since she learned to read at age three and a half. It had been Alicia who'd opened up the world of literature, of books, to Juliana. Alicia had opened up a great deal more than that, Juliana knew, but the gift of reading was the most precious to them both.

And who would've thought, she mused, still impressed by the walls of shelves that started at the floor and led all the way up to the high tin ceiling, filled with books of all topics, shapes and sizes, who would've thought that she would ever own a house that held a library this size?

She took another step into the room, then stopped.

There was a sound. She paused, listening. It was the slow, steady sound of breathing.

It was Webster Donovan, and he was lying on his back on the couch that sat underneath the window. One arm was up over his handsome face, his eyes buried in the crook of his elbow. His other hand rested on his broad chest. Both of his feet were still on the floor, as if he had been too tired to pull them up.

Or as if he knew his worn-out cowboy boots didn't belong on her antique furniture, Juliana grudgingly admitted. So maybe he wasn't *entirely* mannerless, although sleeping like this in one of her public rooms didn't win him any points. The way he was dressed, he looked little better than a vagrant, and his presence would keep the rest of her guests out of the elegant library. And that certainly wasn't fair.

"Mr. Donovan," she said, her voice low but clear.

He didn't move.

Juliana took a step closer. "Mr. Donovan." Louder this time. "Please wake up."

His hand twitched very slightly.

Why was it that Alicia was always off on one of her trips at times like these? Juliana sighed. All right. She was going to have to touch him. So she'd touch his arm, wake him up, then quickly jump out of range.

Another step, and Juliana was close enough to breathe in his masculine scent. Sweet heavens, he smelled good. *But you're not just an animal in heat,* she reminded herself. *This man may be handsome, but he's also conceited, rude, and extremely forward. Even if you wanted a man around—which you don't—you'd never pick this one, not in a million years, despite how good he smells.*

She touched his shoulder tentatively. "Mr. Donovan?"

The man was asleep.

She shook him slightly. No response.

She shook him harder.

His arm came down, but his eyes were still closed. "Aw, honey," he mumbled, turning onto his side. "C'mon back to bed."

Juliana felt her cheeks start to turn red. "Wake up," she said, shaking his shoulder again.

He reached out and caught her hand, pulling it toward his mouth. His lips caressed the delicate pulse at her wrist. Then his tongue tasted the palm of her hand in a wildly intimate gesture. "Babe, you smell so good," he murmured. His voice was low and raspy from sleep.

Juliana pulled her hand away as if she'd been burned. "My name isn't babe. Or honey," she said crossly, wondering how on earth she was going to wake this man up. A cold bucket of water in his face would do wonders for her soul, but the antique couch he was sleeping on and the Oriental rug underneath wouldn't fare quite so well.

"What else am I supposed to call you?" he said softly, and quite lucidly. "You never told me your first name."

He was awake. His blue eyes were open, with more than a touch of amusement in their crystalline depths.

"I would appreciate it if you didn't sleep in the public rooms," she said. Her voice was crisp, businesslike.

He pulled himself into a sitting position, and she took an involuntary step backwards. Which, of course, he noticed.

"I don't bite," he said, then smiled that lazy, infuriating smile of his. "At least not too hard. What *is* your name?" His movements were stiff as he got to his feet.

Suddenly the room seemed much too small. Sweet heavens, the man was tall. "Miss Anderson," Juliana replied. Her soft grey skirt swept behind her as she moved swiftly to the door. "I'll show you your suite."

"You've gotta have a first name," he said, following her out onto the second floor landing. "Everyone's got a first name. What do your parents call you?"

She turned to look at him, her face calm, serene. "I do have a first name," she said, her voice level and emotionless. "But I prefer the guests to call me Miss Anderson."

Web felt a flash of annoyance. God almighty, if she didn't tell him her name, he was going to have to go snooping around that little office he'd seen downstairs. Or spend the next few weeks, not writing as he'd planned, but guessing and imagining her name. Damn, it could be anything. Agnes. Maryanne. Penelope. It could be Jane, for all he knew.

Miss Mystery Name Anderson stopped before an ornate wooden door, pausing to look back at him before she turned the knob.

"I'll give you a key to the room," she said. "You can keep it locked if you want. Most guests don't. But most guests also don't bring their computers on vacation with them."

"I'm not on vacation, Miss Anderson," Web said. She looked away from him as he stressed the formality of her name a little too much. "I'm here to write."

"Yes, that's right," she said, opening the door.

"Miss Dupree told me that you were a writer." He followed her into the room, wishing he could get close enough to her again to breathe in her sweet natural perfume.

What was wrong with him? He wasn't going to get anywhere with this woman by following her around like a lost puppy. And he *was* going to get somewhere with her, he vowed, even if it took all six weeks of his stay.

His eyes fell on the huge bed with the heavy, carved wood headboard and footboard. *That* was exactly where he wanted to end up. In that big bed. With her.

For a moment he could picture her, golden-red curls loose around her face, her body sleek and naked, unfettered by the heavy, restrictive clothing she wore, her lips parted, eager for his kisses, her body moist and ready for him. He'd kiss her slowly, drinking her in, taking his time. He'd trail his lips across her face, her neck, her jawline, and he'd pause at her ear, taking the delicate lobe into his mouth. His breath hot against her, he'd whisper her name—Miss Anderson.

Web laughed out loud, the splendor of his fantasy broken by the sad truth of reality. He really was going to have to find out her first name, he thought, pulling his eyes away from the promise of that big, beautiful bed.

She was looking at him expectantly, waiting for something, her big greenish eyes watching him carefully.

"What sort of things do you write, Mr. Donovan?" she said, obviously repeating the question.

Terrific, he thought. Now she thinks I'm an imbecile.

"I'm trying to write another *New York Times* best seller," he said, "and to live up to the expectations of the critics."

But he still hadn't answered her question.

"Fiction," he finally said. "Is there anything else?

No, don't answer that. Dumb thing to say, particularly for a guy who used to be a journalist.''

A journalist. Juliana felt a flash of uncertainty. There was supposed to be a reviewer from the *Boston Globe* coming out to review 31 Farmer's Hill Road, and his review would be included in a book about New England bed and breakfasts. A good review was worth big money. If Webster Donovan was the reviewer, they'd already gotten off to a shaky start.

But what kind of reviewer would come and stay for six weeks? No, it couldn't be Webster Donovan. Besides, he was obviously prejudiced toward writing fiction.

"I've laid towels out in the bathroom," Juliana said, feeling the silence in the room drag on a bit too long as she stood there examining him from the tips of his scuffed boots to the top of his curly mop of dark hair. "Let me know if you need extras."

She crossed to one of two closed doors and opened it. "Bathroom's here," she said. She opened the other door. "Here's your sitting room."

The second room was as large as the bedroom, but the wallpaper was a green print. Even the ceiling was papered with a matching design. The curtains were cream lace, and they let in the bright October sun. There was a table in front of the bay windows, just the right size for his computer.

Yeah, he was going to like working here.

"Both of the fireplaces work," she said. "If it gets cold enough, I'll light a fire in the evening, if you plan to be in."

There were two easy chairs in front of the green tiled fireplace, a huge, ornately framed mirror above it. The rug, the antique furniture, the wallpaper, everything about the room was right out of the late nineteenth century. It was perfect.

"You did a good job decorating," he said, looking

back into the bedroom. That big bed had caught his attention so totally, he hadn't even noticed the color of the walls until now. It wasn't quite pink, but it was close. Dusty rose, he guessed it would be called. The spread on the bed matched the wallpaper, and the wall was papered in the tripartite style—divided into three sections with three different patterns of the same colors. The bedroom ceiling, too, was papered, in a different, lighter print. The woodwork in the room had been painted white.

A quick glance back at the sitting room, his office, he already thought of it, revealed natural colored woodworking, polished to a high shine. "This house is a real gem."

"You should've seen it when I first bought it." Her smile transformed her face, making her even more beautiful.

She stopped smiling almost immediately, as if she were afraid of giving too much of herself away.

"If you wouldn't mind coming downstairs, Mr. Donovan," she said, "I have some forms for you to fill out."

Again, he followed her, this time back down the glistening oak staircase. "The guest rooms are all on the second floor," she said in a voice like a tour guide's. "You've found the library—"

"And the kitchen," he said. "This is a terrific house. Is it Anabel?"

"What?" The non sequitur caught her off guard.

He was smiling at her. "Or maybe Briana. That fits your hair." He reached out to brush a rebellious curl off her face.

Juliana took a step backward, impatience on her face. "Please respect the other guests' privacy. As I said before, many of them don't bother locking their doors when they go out."

His grin widened, revealing straight, white teeth.

"Yeah," he said. "No problem. Let's see, *A . . . B . . . C . . .* Cassandra?"

"All of the guest rooms are on the second floor." She tried to ignore him. "Here on the first floor, I'd appreciate it if you'd restrict yourself to using only the front parlor, the living and dining rooms, and the kitchen. Oh, there is a small water closet down here, too."

"What's on the third floor?" he asked.

"My apartment," she said, turning away from him to sweep into the small office.

Web glanced back toward the staircase. Her apartment. "Oh," he said.

"It's off limits to the guests," she said, sitting behind a delicate antique writing desk. *And* I'm *off limits, too, bub,* she thought darkly, *so stop looking at me as if you're so certain we're going to end up in bed together. Because we're not.* "Miss Dupree has a room on the first floor. That's off limits, too. Now, how do you intend to pay for your room?" she asked, her voice pleasant.

He sat down on the other side of the desk. "Credit card. How about Deanna?"

She blinked.

"What are you doing tonight?" he asked. "Emily?"

"I'm serving dinner to four guests," she said tartly. "Five, if you're interested in joining them."

"Do you eat with the guests like you did at breakfast?" he asked.

"Yes."

"Then I'm interested," he said. "Very interested."

Juliana met his warm gaze evenly. "Mr. Donovan, do you always come on too strong?"

"Miss Anderson," he said, and his husky voice managed to make the formal name sound like an endearment. "You ain't seen nothin' yet."

THREE

Juliana looked at herself critically in the full-length mirror. Her hair was in a very traditional Victorian style, swept up into a pile on top of her head, the front puffed out. She'd managed to get it just right tonight, and her hair, along with her evening gown, made her look like she'd stepped directly from the pages of a history book.

The gown was a copy of a dress that had been made in 1885. It was a deep, rich shade of blue with a low neckline, large puff sleeves and a tight, well-tailored bodice.

She had put on very little makeup, just enough to accent her eyes and put some color in her cheeks and lips. Just enough to make her feel costumed and ready for the performance.

Because, really, that's what it was. A show.

She'd always loved acting and theater, and she often regretted that she'd never had the chance to perform back in high school.

Juliana made a face at herself in the mirror. She'd made an awful lot of mistakes back then, back before she met Alicia. But since that time, she'd learned to forgive herself for all those transgressions. After all, the past wasn't something that could be changed by fretting. Or by regretting, she told herself sternly.

But the future . . . now *that* was something she could control. And as soon as she stopped staring at herself in this mirror, she would go down all those flights of stairs to where her guests were surely waiting in the front parlor, and make sure her future didn't start intersecting with Webster Donovan's. Because she didn't want that kind of future. She didn't have room in her life for a man, especially not a man like Mr. Donovan. No way.

Right now the only future she wanted was the immediate one. She wanted to get through this evening. Tomorrow night she wouldn't be serving dinner, so after breakfast she would have the entire day for herself. She'd take a ride over to the stable and go for a picnic with Captain. Thinking about it was enough to put a smile back on her face.

Locking her apartment door behind her, Juliana went down the stairs, her long skirt rustling as it trailed behind her.

Her voice was low and clear as she entered the front parlor. "Good evening."

The fire she'd made earlier was blazing briskly in the fireplace, the flames sparking and popping as they consumed the dry wood behind the safety screen.

Two of her guests tonight were newlyweds, and they sat together on the couch, oblivious to everyone else in the room. Her other two guests, the elderly Mrs. Bowers and her slightly younger companion, Miss May, sat by the window, playing backgammon.

They both smiled congenially up at her.

"You look lovely tonight, dear," Mrs. Bowers said.

"I'll second that," came a voice from behind her.

"Mr. Donovan," Juliana said coolly, nodding her

head in greeting and in gracious acknowledgement of his compliment as she turned to look back at him.

She couldn't keep her eyes from widening when she saw him.

Gone were the worn-out, greasy clothes, the ragged, reckless, windblown look.

Webster Donovan was wearing a tuxedo, looking every inch—and, sweet heavens, there were so *many* inches of him—the perfect, upperclass gentleman. His black jacket and pants had been tailored to his body like a second skin, and he wore them with such a familiarity that Juliana knew he was no stranger to formal clothes. He wore a black bow tie and cummerbund, and a crisp, white shirt. With his cheeks smooth, obviously freshly shaved, and his unruly hair slicked back from his handsome face, he looked sophisticated, debonair. So why was she reminded of a panther about to strike?

He was leaning against the door frame, one long, powerful leg crossed in front of the other at the ankle. His crystal-blue eyes continued to sweep her body and face appreciatively, lingering just a moment too long on her low neckline, on the tops of her breasts, before returning to meet her gaze.

Juliana felt her cheeks flush, and inwardly she cursed her pale complexion. She didn't want to give him the satisfaction of knowing how much he rattled her. Taking a deep breath, she made quick introductions all around. "Shall we go into the dining room?" she then asked. "Mr. Donovan, if you would please escort Mrs. Bowers and Miss May?"

She smiled at him sweetly, knowing that the two older ladies would keep him occupied with their stories and questions until well after the meal. Anderson one, Donovan zero.

But Webster merely inclined his head in acquiescence to her request, and with a slightly mocking smile aimed at Juliana, he offered the ladies his arms.

I'm not even going to wonder *what his smile means,* Juliana told herself. *He only did it to make me wonder.*

But in the kitchen, there was no time to wonder about anything, except the best way to get the food out of the oven and onto the table.

The sumptuous meal passed quickly enough. And Webster Donovan behaved himself quite nicely, Juliana decided. She let her eyes rest on his face as he entertained the entire table with his stories of being a reporter on the presidential campaign back in 1988.

Unlike many people who could tell a good tale, Mr. Donovan was also a good listener. He paid close attention, with genuine interest in his eyes, as Mrs. Bowers talked about her life as a young bride during the Second World War. He even got Miss May to give him more than her normal monosyllabic answers as he gently asked about her beloved bird-watching trips.

The newlyweds were lost in each other, and Webster even knew enough to let them remain distant. Mr. Donovan, Juliana quickly corrected herself. She couldn't start thinking of him as Webster. That was far too dangerous.

He glanced across the table at her, as if he knew she was thinking about him. Trapped for a moment, she stared back into his eyes—eyes that nearly pierced her with their determination, eyes that didn't bother to hide his desire for her.

Juliana quickly turned away. It would be too easy to be drawn in by this man, much too easy. But smooth-talking, sophisticated, handsome men who thought they were God's gift to women just weren't her style. Except suddenly she had a very vivid picture of Webster Donovan standing in her kitchen, his deep-blue eyes soft and vulnerable, his face confused, all of that hard edge gone. She wondered for a moment if that had been an illusion or an act. Or was that man she'd seen for one brief moment in her kitchen hidden somewhere under the slick, smooth facade?

You're not going to find out, she told herself firmly. *Just keep your distance, be polite, and make sure there's always an elderly guest or two around when he's in the room.*

It wasn't long after Juliana had poured out cups of coffee and tea that the newlyweds excused themselves.

"Shall we go into the parlor?" Juliana asked then, smiling at Mrs. Bowers and Miss May. "How does a glass of brandy sound?"

The two older ladies exchanged a somewhat mischievous glance, then smiled coyly at Mr. Donovan. "Not tonight, dear," Mrs. Bowers said. "Eloise and I are tired from our long drive. We thought we'd turn in early."

"I'd love a glass of brandy," Webster said, sending a quick wink over to the two smiling ladies.

Sweet heavens, it was a conspiracy, Juliana realized. It must have happened when she was in the kitchen. Webster Donovan now had her other guests working with him in some diabolical plot to get her alone.

Change that score, she thought. Donovan managed to come out on top, not only by handling the dinner guests graciously, but also by using the situation to his advantage. Donovan two, Anderson one. Gritting her teeth, she still managed to smile politely.

"Then I'll bid you good night, ladies," she said, her voice calm as usual. She turned to Webster. "If you'll just give me a moment to clear the table and get the glasses before I join you in the front parlor? Perhaps you wouldn't mind stoking the fire."

Poor word choice. Juliana realized it the instant the words were out of her mouth.

He nodded back at her, equally polite, but his eyes said, "I'll stoke your fire any day, baby."

She fled into the kitchen. Argh! This man was going

to drive her crazy. Six weeks was . . . sweet heavens! Forty-two days!

It only took a few minutes to clear off the big oak table, but Juliana dawdled, taking her time. Finally she'd done as much as she could. She wasn't dressed to wash the dishes, and she didn't want to risk water spots on the fine blue material of her gown.

Slowly she took two brandy snifters down from the cabinet. She almost put one back, then silently berated herself. She *wanted* to have some brandy, damn it, and it wasn't fair that this great, huge, oversized, obviously oversexed, way too macho, male person should make her feel uncomfortable in her own house. *Double* damn it.

Still seething, she carried the two glasses toward the front parlor. But she stopped in the doorway, looking in.

Webster Donovan stood in front of the fireplace, arm outstretched, braced against the mantel, head bent to stare down into the glowing flames. He hadn't heard her at the door, and his face had a soft, pensive, yearning look.

Juliana almost didn't go in. This was the kind of man she couldn't defend herself from. This quiet, thoughtful, uncertain Webster could get right under her skin. Maybe he already had, she thought with an icy shiver of apprehension.

But he looked up then and spotted her standing there. And the edge came back into his eyes.

Juliana smiled, realizing at that moment that he was his own worst enemy. He wanted her—he had made that more than clear—but as long as he played the part of the worldly, sarcastic, overeager lothario, he didn't stand a chance with her.

"Ooh, a smile," he said. "Be still my heart."

She crossed to the heavy oak sideboard and took the bottle of brandy from the cabinet. "Did you get much work done today, Mr. Donovan?" she asked politely, pouring the amber-colored liquid into the snifters. Crossing back toward the fireplace, a glass in each hand, she held one out to him.

Juliana braced herself as he reached to take the glass from her. As she expected, he purposely let their hands touch. His fingers were warm and solid, and she staunchly ignored the quickening of her pulse.

"I set up my computer," he said, answering her question, "and I took about a six-hour nap."

Webster watched as she gracefully sat down in one of the easy chairs that faced the fireplace. She swirled the brandy in her glass, heating it with the warmth of her hand.

Firelight played across her features as she stared into the flames. Her face was accented by wide cheekbones, a firm chin, a small straight nose with a smattering of freckles. Her eyebrows were delicate arches, her lashes long and thick. Her eyes were . . . blue? They'd been the most wonderful mix of blue, green, and golden brown this morning when he'd held her in his arms.

She turned toward him, and he saw a flash of green and gold in her eyes. "Mr. Donovan, won't you sit down?" she said. "You're impossibly tall to start with, and if you insist on standing, my neck won't survive this conversation."

Web lowered himself into another easy chair with a smile. "Impossibly tall? I'm only six five. I played college basketball, and I was the runt of the team. Now, *those* guys were impossibly tall. Tell me, is it Janet?" he asked, out of the blue.

She laughed, and Webster felt a thrill of triumph race through his veins. "Are we starting *this* game again?" she asked. She had a smile, a real, genuine smile on her lips, not one of those very polite, Victorian half smiles.

"What do you do for fun up here?" he asked. "Jennifer?"

"Me in particular?" she asked, ignoring his second question. "Or do you mean 'you' in general?"

"You in particular. Is your name Jane?"

Another laugh, and it was frighteningly musical. Webster had that peculiar tight feeling in his chest again.

"I bake bread," she said. "I sing in the church choir, I go riding. I own a gelding, he's stabled about four miles down the road."

"A gelding?" he said, the firelight making his black hair glisten. His lips curved in a smile. "I would have thought a woman like you would have a stallion."

Double entendre time again, Juliana thought. *Fine, two could play this game*. "Stallions can be more trouble than they're worth, Mr. Donovan," she said.

She met his eyes steadily, and he laughed.

"Tell me, what else do you like to do?" he said. "Besides ride your horse?"

"I love books," Juliana said. "My aunt and I are always reading something. We particularly like mysteries, you know, who-dun-its."

"Well, there you go," Web said, his teeth flashing in the dim light. "You read books, I write 'em. We're a perfect match."

Juliana took a sip of the brandy, feeling it warm her all the way down to her stomach. She raised one eyebrow skeptically. "What exactly are you writing, Mr. Donovan?"

Not Mr. Donovan, *Webster*, he thought. He wanted to hear her say his name.

"Well, to be perfectly honest," he said, and she glanced over at him. His slick facade was still carefully in place. His words were only an expression; he had no intention of being perfectly honest at all. "I'm planning to make this second book another contemporary western," he said. "I haven't actually started writing yet. I've kind of been procastinating, which is why I came out here. I'm trying to break my pattern of fooling around and get going with the work."

"So you set up your computer, then take a six-hour nap in the middle of the day?"

He laughed, but it was a touch too hearty. "Trust me, that wasn't procrastination. It was survival. I hadn't slept in over two days. I get . . . dangerous when that happens."

She had noticed.

With a shower of sparks, a log fell out of the confines of the andirons onto the bricks of the hearth.

Webster put his glass down and removed the screen. He knelt down and used the fire iron to wrestle the log back up into the fire. He stayed there on the rug in front of the fire, sitting at Juliana's feet. "So when do you have a night off?" he asked. "When can I take you out to dinner or dancing or a movie—or anything?"

He could hear her skirt rustle quietly as she shifted position in the chair. "I'm sorry, Mr. Donovan," she said softly, "but I don't go out with guests."

True, none had ever asked her before, since most of her guests were happily married or old enough to be her grandfather. But it seemed like a good policy. It *was* a good policy. She knew it was.

"Oh, come on," he said, turning to face her, still sitting on the floor. "I'm just talking about a date. Very harmless."

She looked back at him steadily. "What's harmless to you isn't necessarily harmless to someone else, Mr. Donovan."

"God, will you *please* call me Web."

A curly lock of dark hair had fallen across his forehead. He was still on the floor, looking up at her with frustration in his eyes.

It was the first genuine emotion she'd seen in his

face since she'd come into the room, and it almost made her change her mind. Almost.

She stood up. "Mr. Donovan," she said. "I've been running this bed and breakfast for nearly five years. I believe I know what's best, particularly in dealing with a guest who intends to remain for over a month. If that makes you unhappy, you should feel free to check out at any time."

Webster Donovan stood up, too. "Whoa, baby, relax—"

"I do *not* appreciate being called 'baby,'" Juliana said.

He ran his fingers through his hair with impatience. "If you told me your name, I wouldn't *have* to call you baby."

"I repeat, I prefer Miss Anderson."

"Yeah, well, I *don't*. Look, I know your name starts with a *J*."

She stared at him, startled. "How do you know that?"

"I looked through your mail," he said with a shrug. He didn't even have the decency to blush.

"Are you always rude and offensive, Mr. Donovan," Juliana said, her eyes flashing, "or is there something about me that brings this out in you?"

He took a step toward her. "Oh, come on—"

"I'd appreciate it if you'd keep your distance," she said, backing away.

Webster was caught off guard. "Whoa!" he said. "Wait a minute! It's not like I'm going to attack you or anything."

"No? You did this morning." Even as Juliana said it, she realized that it wasn't quite fair. He *hadn't* attacked her, but sweet heavens, she was mad at him.

Webster's jaw tightened. "I don't need to *attack* women, *Miss Anderson*," he said angrily. "They usually just fall into my arms, the way *you* did this morning.''

Oh boy, Webster thought, he'd made her angry now. If the lightning bolts that just shot out of her eyes had been real, he'd be a dead man.

"You are *such* a jerk," she said, the Victorian woman replaced by a late-twentieth-century righteous feminist.

Spinning on her heels, she swept toward the parlor door with great dignity and left the room.

Juliana stormed up to her apartment, locking the door tightly behind her. She wouldn't put it past him to follow her, the rude, arrogant . . . *man!*

She quickly changed out of her gown, hanging it carefully in the closet. Rummaging through her dresser drawers, she pulled out a running bra and a pair of bike shorts. She dressed, then slipped her feet into her running shoes.

With the exception of her tiny kitchen and the bathroom, her apartment was one vast, opened-up, modern-looking room. Because it was the third floor, the ceiling was at all kinds of angles and there were all sorts of nooks and crannies.

Her big bed was tucked into a cozy alcove at one side of the room. She had a comfortable couch, her VCR, TV and stereo system set up in another corner. But now she went to a third area, where she kept her workout equipment.

She had an exercise bike, a stairmaster, and a rowing machine. Slipping a CD into her Walkman, she strapped on her belt, and adjusted the headphones. She climbed onto the exercise bike, set it for level eight, and took out her frustrations.

FOUR

Webster Donovan was still in a bad mood.

He wasn't writing.

He *was* trying, practically chaining himself to his computer, but nothing would come out. Nothing worth saving, anyway.

He'd spent the past two days locked in his room. Juliana hadn't even had a chance to go in and clean up. He was always there. Sitting at his computer. Not writing.

Tuesday morning, he was the only guest in the house. At nine o'clock, Juliana got tired of waiting for him to come down for breakfast, so she took a tray of food upstairs to his room. She put her ear to the door, and she could hear the sound of his computer keyboard clacking.

She knocked softly, and he came to the door almost immediately.

He wore only a pair of baggy sweatpants. No shirt, no shoes. His body was long and lean, and still carried the darkness of his summertime tan. His shoulders were broad and rock solid, his chest was powerful, and his stomach a washboard of well-defined muscles.

A wild jumble of curls fell over his forehead, as if he'd run his hands through his hair over and over. The laughter lines in his face were deepened from fatigue, and his eyes were rimmed with red.

He stared at her blankly.

"I brought your breakfast up," she said, suddenly embarrassed, not by his half-nakedness, but because she had bothered him. "I'm sorry I interrupted your writing."

Webster shook his head tiredly, a rueful smile touching the edges of his mouth. "No, I was only writing a letter to my agent."

He had to ask his agent to contact his publisher to extend the due date of this second book. He couldn't finish it in time. How could he finish it when he couldn't even start it?

Juliana held out the tray, then took a step backwards after he took it from her.

"I'm going into town," she said. "Is there anything I can pick up for you?"

He carried the tray into the other room, and she was forced to follow him. She tried not to look at his smooth, bare back or at the way his sweat pants rode low on his slim hips.

Instead, she looked at the room. It was an outrageous mess. Half-empty cups of coffee were balanced on every available surface, and corn chips spilled out of several open bags. Clothes were scattered everywhere, and loose paper was everywhere else, along with reference books. A dictionary was held open by a donut on a napkin.

The bed, however, was perfectly made, as if he hadn't slept in it. And looking at him, she realized that was exactly the case. He *hadn't* slept since . . . when was the last time she made up the bed? Sunday afternoon. Today was Tuesday.

"Mr. Donovan," she said. "I would have given you

a break on the price if I'd known you only wanted the breakfast half of the package.''

Webster snorted. It was almost a laugh.

"Need anything?" she asked again.

He looked up at her tiredly from where he sat at the table. "I need a muse," he said. "But that's not something you can pick up at the Star Market."

He took a bite of his pancakes, and Juliana turned to leave. His voice stopped her. "This is really delicious. Thanks for bringing it up."

"You're welcome," she said, surprised.

She turned to leave again, but turned back. "I'm going out today, and I probably won't return until late tonight," she said. "Feel free to use the kitchen."

He nodded, and she left, closing the door gently behind her.

He brought his plate over to the computer and tried to go back to work. But all he could think of were women's names that started with the letter J.

Sometime later, the sound of a motorcycle engine cut through his musing. He stood up, stretching, feeling his tightened muscles scream with neglect as he moved to the window.

Out on the street he could see a powerful black Harley Davidson kicking into higher gear, moving toward town. The rider was tall and slim, wearing tight-fitting blue jeans, a black leather jacket, black cowboy boots and a shiny black helmet.

Webster caught a glimpse of what looked like glistening red-gold hair coming out the back of the helmet, and he pushed his face to the window, hoping for another look.

Red-gold hair? Could it possibly . . . ?

Not possible, Webster thought. Simply not possible.

Juliana pushed the Harley harder, glad there were no other cars or bikes out.

The sun was shining through the few brightly colored leaves that still adorned the trees. The dry leaves that had fallen onto the road were swept up behind her motorcycle, creating a comet-tail effect as she buzzed along the country road.

She needed to think, and she knew just where to go.

She made the sharp right turn onto the gravel driveway leading up to the stable.

It didn't take long to get Captain saddled up.

He was as eager to run as she was, and she took him up to the pasture. With only a light touch of her heels, Captain was off, streaking across the field.

Juliana felt herself relax, felt her body move with the big horse's rhythm. Nothing mattered but right now, and right now was pretty darn good.

Captain stretched out, and she let him take the jump at the end of the field. It was only a small stone wall, and he cleared it easily. Juliana pulled the horse back as they entered the woods, following the dirt path that took them further up the side of the mountain.

Captain wanted to have a snack of the leaves that grew in the bushes by the side of the trail, but Juliana kept a firm hand on the reins. "Come on, Captain," she said, and his ears flickered in response to her musical voice. "You're a horse, not a goat."

They settled into a comfortable walk, taking their sweet time. The air was cool, but the sun was warm where it penetrated the thinning leaves of the trees. When they reached the top of the climb, Juliana reined Captain in, and they both stood there, looking down the mountain.

She could see the steeple of the congregational church poking above the canopy of red, orange, gold, and brown leaves. She could see the town hall, and the clearing where the village green lay. She turned her head, following the line of the road. She could see the roof of Liz and Sam Beckwith's huge house, and wondered again how such a modern home could blend so well with the countryside. She could also see the bright-green roof of five-year-old Jamey's plastic Sesame Street playhouse. She smiled, remembering Liz's and her small daughter's twin looks of shock when Sam brought that little playhouse home the first time. Except Liz was shocked by the horrendous colors, while little Jamey was shocked with sheer joy.

Liz was pregnant with her third child, and she was due in little less than a month.

"I've got to stop over there on my way home," Juliana murmured to Captain.

Her eyes traveled a bit further down the road, and she found the familiar crockets, finials, and weathervanes that bedecked the roof of her huge, old Victorian monstrosity. The cream-colored gingerbread trim stood out against the dark blue of the house, the large windows reflecting the bright sunlight. If she squinted, she could see the oriel windows of Webster's sitting room.

"What am I doing, Captain?" Juliana groaned. "I'm spending far too much time and energy thinking about this man. I don't even like him. He's so obnoxious."

So why couldn't she stop thinking about the way he'd held her? Why, even when he was his most infuriating, did she want to run her fingers through his wild, dark hair?

Captain snorted, glancing up at the slim woman on his back.

"Yeah," she agreed. "It's hormones. And maybe if I'm lucky it'll pass. C'mon, boy."

Gently pulling the reins, she turned Captain around and headed back down the mountain.

Liz Beckwith looked as if she had an enormous watermelon underneath her dress. Her arms and legs were still slender, her ankles and fingers unswollen. She really looked as if she were playing at being pregnant, rather than mere weeks away from delivery.

Her short blond hair curled about her pixie face, and she smiled at Juliana from her rocking chair. "Spill it," she demanded.

Juliana shrugged. "Nothing's new."

Liz made a face. "Last time *I* looked in the dictionary, the definition for nothing didn't include a six-and-a-half-foot tall hunk of man with curly dark hair and a red Miata. *How* does he fit inside that tiny car?"

Juliana shook her head in mock sadness. "You've been spying on me."

Her friend giggled. "Can't you just see me, waddling through the woods, a pair of binoculars around my neck, quiet as a lumbering hippo?"

"Yes."

"The man *must* have a name."

Juliana nodded. "Webster Donovan."

Liz sat up, her light blue eyes widening. "Webster Donovan, the *author*?"

Juliana nodded again. "He's trying to write his second book as we speak. I think he's got writer's block or something. He spends most of his time stomping around his room," Juliana said. "Sometimes I feel like telling him to find another job."

"Oh, but, no! Jule, his first book was *great*," Liz enthused. "It's called *Out of Time*. Have you and Alicia read it?"

"No."

"Oh, wow, you're gonna love it. I'll lend it to you." Liz pushed herself out of the rocking chair and moved with surprising grace toward a huge bookshelf that covered most of the living room wall. "Oh, darn. It's on one of Sam's shelves." The tiny woman pointed up to the very top shelf. "Push a chair over—"

"I'm not going to let you climb up there," Juliana said, warningly.

Liz gave her an "of course I wouldn't" look. "*You* climb up, oh tall one. It's the book with the red cover, let's see, one, two, three, four, five . . . eighth from the end."

Juliana stood on her tiptoes on the dining room chair. She pointed to the book, and Liz nodded. "That's the one."

Pulling the heavy book from the shelf, Juliana wiped the dust from the top.

Taking it eagerly, Liz sat down on the edge of the coffee table, opening it to the first page. As Juliana carried the chair back to the dining room, she listened to Liz read the first few paragraphs of the book.

It was a description of a man alone in a ghost town, and the words flowed beautifully, creating a poetry and a poignance that made Juliana want to hear more.

But Liz stopped reading, turning to the back of the dust cover, to the black and white picture of Webster Donovan.

"No," Liz said flatly, shaking her blond curls. "This guy is simply too good looking. He must have some fatal flaw."

Juliana slipped the book into her backpack, only glancing at the photo. Webster looked much better in real life. "Well, let's see. He's rude, arrogant, conceited, and way too pushy."

Liz laughed. "Jule, you just described *Sam*." She leaned forward, her eyes sparkling with mischief. "So when are you going out with him?"

"I'm not."

"Jule . . ."

"I'm *not*."

"Jule . . ."

"Alicia has lived nearly eighty years without a man, and if she can do it, I can, too."

Liz was silent for a long time, her hands pressed to her swollen belly as the little life inside pushed against her, stretching and turning within the confines of her womb. For once her face was serious as she looked at Juliana.

She said, "Maybe Alicia just never found the right man."

FIVE

Juliana looked up from the tiny table in the bar as Liz sat down next to her.

"They're going to start playing soon," the small blond woman said, watching the stage where her husband and his band had set up their instruments. "You know, I met Sam here at Red's."

Juliana's green eyes danced with unconcealed delight. "I didn't know," she said.

"It'll be exactly ten years ago in January."

Liz and Sam's son Chris had just turned nine last week. "You mean, since you've been married?" Juliana asked.

Liz grinned. "No. I mean, since we met. We, um, took one look at each other and, well, shall I say . . . got busy?"

Juliana laughed, shaking her head in disbelief. "How come you never told me this before?"

"I was waiting for the right moment," Liz said. "You know, Sam and I have only been married for seven years. Sam didn't even know Chris existed until he was almost two."

"You didn't tell him?"

"I couldn't find him! He was just some guitar-playing drifter who sat in with the house band one Saturday night. We didn't make each other any promises—or take any precautions. He only stayed for three days, but I was head over heels in love with him. I never told him, though. I was afraid to.

"Finally, he left for Nashville, and I joined the ranks of the single parents of America. I made a few half-hearted attempts to get in touch with him, but I wasn't even sure he'd remember my name.

"Then one evening, a couple years later, I was just sitting at home, watching the tube, and the Country Music Awards were on. And who wins the award for writing the song of the year? Sam Beckwith. And he played his song, and it was about some guy who meets a woman in a bar, leaves her behind, and always regrets it. He makes the big time, and he realizes that he'd give it all up for the chance to go back and live that part of his life over, do it differently, because even after all that time, he's still in love with her. And when Sam stood up to get that award, he looked directly into the camera, held up that big crystal prize and said, 'Liz, if you're out there, I'm still dreaming about you, darlin'.' " Liz imitated Sam's deep voice perfectly. "Chris and I were in Nashville within twenty-four hours. Sam and I got married, and, see? Now we're living happily ever after."

"That's a wild story," Juliana said. Her green eyes narrowed. "Why are you telling it to me now?"

"Nostalgia." Liz shrugged. "Being here in Red's brings it all back."

Juliana crossed her arms, her face very skeptical. "Oh, really? And the twenty-five other times we've been here together haven't been sufficiently nostalgic? Come on, Liz," she said. "Let's have it. Is there some not-so-subtle message I'm supposed to be getting?"

The shorter woman smiled sheepishly. "All right.

My point is, at one time I was convinced that I'd never be happy. I was desperately in love with Sam, and I couldn't even *find* him, and it just seemed really likely that I'd spend the rest of my life alone. But I didn't. It worked out. I just don't think you should be so *positive* that you're not going to find some nice, six-and-a-half-foot tall guy—''

Juliana rolled her eyes. "Liz . . ."

"—to spend the rest of your life with."

"Who've you got Jule paired off with now, Lizzie?"

Kurt Pottersfield slid a chair over to their table, and both women greeted him with a kiss.

"Forget it," Juliana said quickly. "How's crime fighting going, Sheriff?"

Liz's brother Kurt was the only law-enforcement official in all of Benton County. His uniform looked out of place in the crowded bar, but everybody knew him and greeted him warmly as they passed by.

"Did I hear you say six and a half feet *tall*?" he asked Liz.

"Yeah, shorty," she teased her brother. "Jule's new guest. He's a famous, *tall* author."

Kurt was movie-star handsome, with thick brown hair, hazel eyes, and an almost too-pretty face. He was also movie-star height, standing five feet seven inches in his boots.

Kurt grinned. "With you around, sprout, I'll never be the shortest. Besides, last time I checked, I was almost as tall as Jule."

The music started—a solid, down-home country two-step. Sam's long fingers flew up and down the frets and across the strings of his guitar.

"Yee-hah!" Kurt shouted.

Juliana smiled at Liz. "That husband of yours sure can play." She turned to Kurt. "You on or off duty, lawman?"

"Off duty and ready to be your dancin' fool." Kurt grinned, standing and offering Juliana his hand.

She pulled her sweater over her head and threw it on the chair next to Liz as she took Kurt's hand.

"Order me a tallboy, sis," he shouted back over his shoulder.

The dance floor was already packed and hotter than blazes from the lights. Sam winked at Juliana from the stage as she began to dance with Kurt, and she smiled back at him, thinking about Sam and Liz's rocky start. All those years of unhappiness could have been avoided, she thought, if only they'd been able to communicate right from the very beginning. They'd both loved each other, but neither one of them had thought to tell the other.

Inwardly she shook her head, thinking of her own disastrous near marriage. In Juliana's case, the trouble only began *after* she and her fiancé, Dennis, started communicating. No, Liz's story was sweet and touching, but the fact remained that Juliana couldn't hope for something she was never going to have. And there'd be plenty of time to cry over *that* when she was alone in her apartment, late at night.

Juliana smiled into Kurt's pretty hazel eyes, and he spun her around and around the floor until she was nearly giddy with dizziness and laughter.

Web started the engine of his little car, holding the cold steering wheel carefully. He was feeling dizzy, a little warm, and more than a little off balance.

Food, he thought. He needed some food in his stomach; that would make him feel better.

He pointed his car toward town, but before he reached the quaint little green with its border of shops and restaurants, he saw a sign for a place called Red's. It was not your upperclass establishment, but there were so many cars out in the parking lot, Web figured *some-*

thing had to be going on inside that was worth checking out. A neon sign in the front window said, Good Food, Good Drinks. Good enough.

The club was dark inside, and a band was up on the stage. A country band, Web noticed, and they were damn decent, too. The place was a real dive, but it was packed nearly wall to wall with people dancing, laughing, drinking, and listening to the band. Man, thought Webster, if this is Benton, Massachusetts, on a Tuesday night, what are weekends like?

He sidled up to the bar and caught the bartender's eye, signaling for a beer. The mug came frosted, and Web took a quick sip as he ordered a turkey sandwich on rye. He sat back on the bar stool then and nursed his beer as he watched the band.

They finished a song, and the crowd roared its approval. The lead guitar player immediately kicked into another song, one Web recognized. It was a Sam Beckwith tune from a few years ago, back when the country singer was just starting his legendary climb to fame.

Man, this guy could play *and* sing just like Beckwith. Webster squinted, staring hard at the man in the black cowboy hat who stood center stage in front of a mike.

The barkeep tapped him on the shoulder. "One turkey on rye. You wanna pay now or run a tab?"

"Tab," Web answered, and pointed to the stage. "Hey, is that—?"

The burly bartender grinned. "Sam Beckwith. In person."

"What the hell is he doing playing here?" Web asked, astonished. Beckwith could fill the Meadowlands Arena at twenty bucks a head. "No offense . . ."

The other man grinned. "None taken. Sam lives down the road. When he's in town, he likes to show off for that pretty little wife of his. I can't complain. Oh, yeah, I should warn you—Sam's wife's pregnant, so he doesn't want anyone smoking in here tonight. You want a butt, take it outside."

"This is wild," Webster said, taking a bite of his sandwich. "Absolutely wild."

He finished his sandwich and polished off several more mugs of beer as he watched the band. Sam Beckwith in person, he thought, shaking his head in disbelief. Playing in a club that was smaller than his parents' living room . . .

There was a dance floor down in front of the stage, and as the band kicked into a swing tune, most of the dancers moved aside, leaving plenty of room for a man and a woman who were doing some fancy jitterbug moves.

The woman was a knockout, dressed in slim-fitting jeans that accentuated her slender hips and small waist. She wore a black tank top that fit like a glove over her full breasts and torso. Her hair was the most marvelous red-gold color, and it seemed to explode around her face—

Webster stood up, leaving his beer half finished and forgotten on the bar. He pushed his way through the crowd. God almighty—it *was* her.

It was Miss Anderson.

But it was a Miss Anderson *he'd* never seen before.

Damn, she looked good enough to eat. Her legs were *so* long. He'd known that somewhere underneath all those skirts lurked a fabulous pair of legs. And, oh Lord, the woman had a tattoo! It was a tiny little one, a teensy little rose by her left shoulder blade, peeking out from the racer back of her tank top.

Her long, slender arms were exposed, and he realized that with the exception of her low-cut evening gown, which she'd only worn that one night, she'd always kept herself carefully and modestly covered. It seemed erotic, risque even, for her to show so much of her skin, here in a bar, in a public place. With a start, he realized that it was only her arms that were bare. Her *arms*, for crying out loud. Yet he was more turned on by the sight of her arms than he'd ever been even when he'd been surrounded by women in thong bathing suits at the beach.

Her hair was long and loose, and it shimmered in the lights. She was laughing, her beautiful mouth open in a smile of pleasure, her eyes sparkling as she looked at the man she was dancing with.

The man she was dancing with, Webster realized suddenly, was a uniformed policeman. No, he was the town sheriff, he corrected himself, catching a glimpse of the man's badge. Worse and worse. This sheriff was also quite possibly the most handsome man in the entire bar—and Web included both himself and Sam Bethwith in that tally. Whatever points Webster won for being taller, he lost them for not being able to dance as well as the shorter man.

Damn, he thought. *No wonder she didn't want to go out with me*.

He thought back to the evening he'd managed to get her alone with him in front of the fireplace. That was the evening he'd planned to seduce her. She'd been as attracted to him as he was to her. He'd known. It was just a matter of finesse, he'd thought, just a matter of getting her in the right place at the right time.

How wrong had he been?

Instead of making love, he'd found himself arguing with the woman.

And now, watching her like this, he realized that he'd give almost anything just to talk to her, just to stand next to her. But judging from the way she'd left his room so quickly today, she didn't want anything to do with him.

The song ended, and Miss Anderson and the sheriff came laughingly, breathlessly to a stop. Instead of giving her a kiss, the sheriff lifted a hand and they high-fived.

Webster felt a wild flash of hope. They didn't kiss. They didn't *kiss*.

The sheriff leaned close to Miss Anderson's ear, she nodded, and he headed toward the back, toward the men's room. And she walked straight toward Webster.

Web knew the exact moment she spotted him there in the crowd. Her eyes met his, widened slightly, and she stopped dead in her tracks. Something, some unknown force propelled him forward, toward her, and she wet her lips nervously.

"Hi," he said. God almighty, did he really just say, "hi," and then grin like an idiot? Smooth, Web, very smooth. *Please God*, he found himself praying, *don't let her see the uncertainty in my eyes. Don't let her know that just being next to her like this scares me to death. And don't let me say something stupid, something that will make her angry at me again.*

She was still breathing heavily from the up-tempo dance, and Webster tried not to watch her chest as it rose and fell. He wanted to pull her into his arms, to feel her body against his.

"I thought you'd be at the house, trying to write," she said, her clear voice cutting through the din of the bar.

"Yeah, no," he said, "I'm not. I'm . . . I'm here."

She smiled at him then. "I noticed."

She was so beautiful his teeth hurt. And he wanted to touch the smooth skin of her arms so badly he felt like some kind of deviant.

"Dance with me?" he asked. His voice was husky, and he cleared his throat. "Please?"

Juliana hesitated. She'd caught a look at Sam's set list and recognized the tune the band was going to play next. It was another fast song. She could handle that.

Couldn't she? She glanced up at the stage. As soon as the rhythm guitar player changed a broken string . . .

"Please?" he said again.

She risked a glance at him.

He was wearing a pair of jeans, a red T-shirt, and his worn-out cowboy boots. His hair was in its usual state of disarray, and his face was tired. His eyes looked almost bruised from lack of sleep, yet she felt herself drawn in by their dark-blue depths.

The crystal edge that was usually in his eyes was missing. Whether it was from fatigue or from some other reason, she didn't know but all of his cocky arrogance was gone. He seemed uncertain, scared even, and to Juliana, the effect was irresistible.

"Okay," she heard herself say. "One dance. Just promise you won't be a jerk."

"I promise." He smiled, like a kid given free rein in a toy store.

"Don't get any ideas," Juliana warned him. "It's just one dance. Do you understand?"

"Yeah," he said. "But don't you think you should tell me your name? I mean, as long as we're gonna dance . . ."

The crowd began to cheer, and she turned her head, pretending not to hear him over the racket.

Up on stage, Sam Beckwith had stepped up to the microphone. "I've just been given a message from Liz, my wife," he said in his thick Kentucky accent. "Y'all know she'll be making me a daddy for the third time 'round in a few more weeks?"

The crowd roared its approval. Webster barely heard a thing as he reached out and brushed a stray curl from Miss Anderson's face. She pulled away from the contact as if he'd burned her.

"Liz asked if I wouldn't mind playing her favorite song right now," Sam continued. "Right this very second, in fact. Liz, darlin', your wish is my command."

The band started the song—a slow, pulsing ballad, not the fast song Juliana had expected. She shook her head in despair. "I'm gonna *kill* that woman," she muttered. She caught sight of Liz standing in the crowd, giving her the thumbs up sign. Juliana resisted the urge to flash her friend a very different hand gesture.

Webster slipped one arm around her waist, taking her hand in his and pulling her in close to him as he began to move to the music.

His arms were hard and strong, yet he held her so gently. And, sweet heavens, he still smelled too damn good. Men just shouldn't smell that good, Juliana thought crossly. There should be a law against it.

Their thighs brushed, denim against denim, and Juliana was afraid her heart was going to stop.

"Mr. Donovan, maybe this isn't such a good idea," Juliana breathed. Sweet heavens, being so close to him like this was making her heart pound and her mouth go dry. Another few seconds, and she'd be trembling. And then he'd know how he made her feel, and he'd kiss her. And he'd kiss her again, and he wouldn't stop kissing her until they were both home in his bed.

He brought her hand up to his wide shoulder, near his neck, and slowly, sensuously, ran his fingers along the bare skin of her arm. Caught off guard by the amount of pleasure that swept through her from his light touch, she tightened her own hand around the back of his neck. He took that as an invitation, pulling her even closer to him.

A gentle hand under her chin pulled her face up, and she realized with shock that he wasn't going to wait. He was going to kiss her right then and there. She didn't have time to protest. She didn't have time to pull away. His lips found hers, warm and soft and sweet.

But still she didn't pull away. In fact, she was clinging to him as tightly as he was holding her, and he kissed her harder, deeper, the dancing all but forgotten. She could feel her heart pounding—or was it his?

One large hand pressed her hips against him, and she could feel the hardness of his arousal. Even more shocking was the sudden wave of fire that raced through her. She wanted him as badly as he wanted her.

Somehow she pushed him away. "Stop," she said, breathing hard. "I can't do this."

She turned and was swallowed up by the crowd.

Webster tried to follow her, but the club was dark and packed with people. He fought his way through the mob as he saw a flash of her red-gold hair by the door.

It took far too long to get to the club's entrance, even though most people stepped aside for the huge man with the look of hard determination on his face. By the time he stepped out into the cold, clear night, all that was left for him to see was the taillight of a motorcycle, heading quickly down the road.

Webster parked his car carefully outside the big Victorian house. He was feeling dizzy again, and way too hot. Still, he poked his head into the carriage house that served as a garage, looking for the telltale signs of a motorcycle.

But there was nothing. No sign of a bike of any kind.

A four-wheel-drive pickup truck sat quietly on the far side of the garage, and there was plenty of room for at least three or four other vehicles, too. The floor was swept clean, and gardening tools lined one wall, carefully hung on hooks, everything in its own special place.

Web wasn't even sure what he was looking for. A motorcycle handbook, he guessed. Yeah, sure. A spare carburetor or a second shiny black helmet, hanging on the wall.

Of course, maybe the motorcycle didn't even belong

to Miss Anderson. Before tonight, he never would've pictured the proper, quiet, old-fashioned woman on a bike. But he wouldn't have been able to picture her in jeans, her hair loose, looking like something out of a steamy music video either. That woman, that wild, red-haired beauty he'd held in his arms and kissed in the bar tonight . . . *she* would definitely look at home on a motorcycle. He could imagine her swinging one long blue-jeaned leg over the back of a powerful machine, straddling the black leather of the seat, her hair moving behind her in the wind as she took a corner. . . .

Webster went inside to take a cold, cold shower.

Juliana rested her forehead against Captain's strong neck.

"I don't even *like* the guy," she said, and the horse shifted its feet, snuffling softly. "But every now and then I get a glimpse of something in his eyes, and it's like I'm sucked into this mad whirlpool of emotions. Every time it happens, it's harder to get back out. It scares me to death."

She stroked Captain's soft nose, and his big, brown eyes looked back at her, full of disappointment it seemed. She sighed.

"I know, I can't believe I'm actually attracted to him. He thinks he's so perfect. He thinks all he has to do is smile, and I'll fall at his feet." Juliana shook her head. "You know what the funny part is, Captain?"

The horse didn't try to guess.

"The way that man writes could make me fall at his feet." Just the little bit of Webster's novel that Liz had read to her was enough to make Juliana long to hear more. She couldn't wait until Alicia got home and they could read his book together.

Everything would be easier when Alicia was home. Juliana would feel . . . the word was chaperoned.

Yeah, she wanted to be chaperoned around Webster Donovan.

Webster woke up drenched with sweat. Dawn was just beginning to lighten the sky in the east, and the clock on his bedside table read 6:27. A sound from the yard made him sit up, and he stumbled on the cold floor as he crossed to the window.

It was foggy outside, a thick layer of cloud hugging the ground, swirling in the spotlight that was mounted over the garage door.

He saw her.

She pulled her helmet off, freeing all that beautiful hair. Even in the darkness, even in the mist, it gleamed. She swung her leg off her bike—it was a Harley, and a big one—and pushed it into the garage. She came out a moment later, shutting the door behind her. Her face was pale against the darkness of her black leather jacket.

Web watched her walk toward the house, overcome with pangs of jealousy. Where had she been, out all night like that? A better question yet—*who* had she been with?

He remembered the handsome sheriff, and for the first time in a long time, Webster found himself wishing he was someone else.

He shivered, suddenly freezing cold. His head was pounding, and he felt sick to his stomach. Oh, man, he didn't have time for the flu.

Praying he was having a bad reaction to the food and beer he'd had last night or maybe to the disappointment of knowing that the beautiful and evasive Miss Anderson had spent the night with someone else, Webster crawled back into bed.

Juliana looked at the clock: nine-fifteen.

With the exception of the day before, Webster Donovan was usually done with breakfast by eight, wolfing it down, hardly aware of the food he was putting in his mouth in his haste to get back to his writing. Or nonwriting. Or whatever he was doing up there in his room.

She put the pancake batter back in the refrigerator and briskly climbed the stairs to his door. He better not think she was going to bring a tray up every morning from now on.

Putting her ear to the door, she didn't hear the clatter of his computer keyboard. He was probably asleep.

He'd probably stayed at Red's last night until Sam stopped playing—no doubt some time around three or three-thirty. And he *had* been drinking. She'd tasted the beer when he kissed her.

Juliana closed her eyes, wishing that she didn't remember that kiss so damn clearly.

Someone was knocking on his door.

Webster opened his eyes slowly, confused by the

sunlight streaming in through the windows. His head split open with a pain so intense he nearly shouted out loud.

Morning. It was morning.

He risked opening one eye slightly to look at the clock on his bedside table. If it was morning, why did his clock say 4:12?

And where did he get this headache from hell?

Then he remembered.

It was the flu. It was definitely the flu.

He'd spent most of last night and a good part of this morning in the bathroom on his knees in front of the john, doing the big heave-ho.

He was sick.

His stomach still hurt, and it had been emptied out long ago. God almighty, it felt like someone must have a voodoo doll of him, and they were sticking big, sharp pins right in his gut.

But he didn't know anyone who had it in for him that badly. With the exception of Miss Anderson. And he could only guess at her hobbies. But why not voodoo? Nothing she did could surprise him anymore. He never would have guessed she'd own a Harley, either.

"Mr. Donovan."

He opened both eyes. The vision of her lovely face as she stood next to his bed was well worth the stabbing pain that shot through his skull.

Her hair was pulled back up on top of her head. As usual, there were stray curls that escaped the bun she'd made, and they hung in delicate wisps around her face. She wore a pale-blue blouse today, and a skirt of darker blue. Somewhere under that skirt, Webster knew, were long, long legs. Legs that knew how to grip a man-sized motorcycle . . .

"Did you have too much to drink last night?" she asked, not entirely sympathetic.

Web closed his eyes against a new wave of nausea.

It passed, but when he looked up at her again, he could feel the sheen of perspiration on his face, and he knew that he was shaking.

"I've had far more than my share of hangovers," he said, making an effort to enunciate each word precisely, "but I've never had one that gave me a fever."

Her expression changed slightly, and she reached down toward him. Her hand was cool against his forehead, and he closed his eyes. He could feel her fingers as she brushed his hair back out of his face, and felt his forehead again, then his cheek.

It was worth it, he decided right then and there. He'd gladly have the flu, if it meant she would touch him like that.

"You're burning up," she said, concern in her voice. "Oh, *Webster* . . ."

She realized it the same instant he did. He could tell by the look of shock on her face. She'd called him by his first name! A wave of triumph rocked through him, followed by total brain-numbing nausea. If he didn't move fast, he was going to lose it right in front of mysterious Miss Anderson. And that would be very, *very* uncool.

Web tore back the sheets and blankets, unmindful of the fact that he wore only a pair of briefs, and rocketed for the bathroom.

Juliana brought her cordless phone down from her apartment. She'd changed out of her Victorian clothes into a pair of jeans and a T-shirt, and she'd put her hair back in a single braid.

She paced back and forth in Webster's sitting room, talking to Liz, wondering when—if ever—he was going to open the bathroom door.

"First thing you have to do is take his temperature," Liz, a former nurse, was saying.

"Shouldn't I just bring him over to the county hospital?" Juliana asked, her voice low with worry.

"Jule, he's probably got a little bit of the flu," Liz said. "The hospital wouldn't even admit him."

"But he looks so . . . bad," Juliana said, "and I don't think I've ever felt anyone that hot."

"You're really worried about him," Liz said, delight in her voice. "This is so great—"

"This is *not* great," Juliana nearly shouted. "Liz, I don't know anything about taking care of someone else, particularly a rude, obnoxious man—"

"You have any cola? Or ginger ale?" Liz interrupted. "Ginger ale is better. Let it get a little flat. He definitely needs liquids. But first, hang up and take his temperature. If it's higher than one hundred—"

"I can tell you just from touching him that it's higher than one hundred," Juliana interrupted.

"Then try to get some Tylenol into him. If he can't keep it down, and his temp goes up to one oh three or higher, put him in a cool bath."

"How am I supposed to—"

"Climb in first," Liz snickered. "Something tells me he'll follow you fast enough."

Webster didn't look up as the bathroom door opened. He didn't even open his eyes, he just kept his forehead pressed to the floor tiles.

"I'm going to take your temperature" came her cool, familiar voice. Web felt her presence on the floor next to him. She lifted his head, then lowered it onto her soft lap, and he opened his eyes, staring up at her. Either she'd changed her clothes and her hair, or he was experiencing an alternate reality.

"It's okay," she murmured, smoothing back his hair with one hand as she adjusted the aural thermometer with the other. "Hold still," she said. "This won't take long."

She placed the nozzle of the thermometer in his ear and watched the digital readout as she continued to stroke his head.

"Please," he said, his voice hoarse. "I don't want you to see me like this."

"I don't know why," she said, her face perfectly straight, one delicate eyebrow slightly raised. "Your outfit has a certain charm."

"God almighty," Webster said, wetting his parched lips with his tongue. "You're teasing. You're flirting with me. You must know something I don't. I'm dying, right?"

She laughed, a soft, husky, sexy sound that penetrated his misery and made his chest feel suddenly tighter. With shock, he felt another part of his body respond. He was sicker than a dog—so sick that he could barely lift his head—yet he wanted her. And dressed as he was, or rather undressed, wearing only his shorts, there was no way to hide it. Webster closed his eyes in despair. Why should he settle for mere embarrassment when he could be utterly humiliated?

Juliana looked down at Webster, at her hand still soothingly brushing back his thick, dark hair. She was only touching him because he was sick, she told herself. The fact that she'd frequently imagined running her fingers through his curls had nothing to do with it, nothing at all.

The heat radiating from him was alarming, and his skin felt clammy under her cool fingers.

The thermometer beeped. Thank goodness Alicia had insisted they get one of these, with a large digital readout. Juliana couldn't have read the other kind if her life depended on it. She looked carefully at the numbers. One oh three point seven. That was much too high.

"I'm going to get some Tylenol," she said, "but first let's get you back into bed. Can you sit up?"

"I don't know." He looked up at her, vulnerability on his face. "Why are you helping me?"

Why *was* she helping him?

Juliana sat quietly, looking down into his feverish blue eyes. "Because I know what it's like to be alone," she said.

"I don't know why," he said. "I look at you and I wonder what the hell you're doing all by yourself."

She looked back at him steadily. "I could say the same about you."

"I'm a jerk," he said. "You said so yourself."

"Well, right now, you're a sick jerk, so come on, let's get you into bed."

He let her help him up, and he stumbled out into the bedroom, collapsing on the enormous bed. The sheet she pulled over him felt cool against his skin, and he closed his eyes and drifted.

Time had passed—he wasn't sure how much—when he felt a cool hand on his face. Her hand.

"Come on, Webster." Her voice seemed to come from far away. "Time for some Tylenol."

He opened his mouth and tasted the bitter pills on his tongue. Then came the cool wetness of something— ginger ale, he thought.

The instant he swallowed, he knew it was a terrible mistake.

But she was there, holding something, some kind of basin for him. The ginger ale was forcefully returned, and he continued to retch long after his stomach should have been empty. Finally, he lay back, his eyes watering, his whole body shaking.

"I'm sorry," he whispered over and over, his eyes tightly shut. "I'm sorry."

He felt her wipe his face with a wet cloth. All along he'd been trying to impress her. He was so confident, so sophisticated, so brilliant, so sardonically bored with everything. But he really wasn't any of those things.

He was just a man, trying desperately to live up to someone else's expectations.

Now he had been stripped of everything—his pride, his confidence, his sophistication, his strength. Hell, since he was lying on his back, he was even stripped of his height. He looked up at beautiful Miss Anderson, who was sitting on the edge of the bed. But she wasn't looking at him with the revulsion he expected. Instead, her greenish eyes were soft and warm with concern.

"Thank you," he said, unable to hold her steady gaze. When was the last time he'd said those words and actually meant them, the way he did right now?

"You're welcome," she said. Almost as an afterthought, she added, "Juliana."

"What?"

"My name," she said. Her face was serious, but her lips twitched slightly, as if she were hiding a smile. "It's Juliana. I think we probably know each other well enough now to be on a first-name basis, don't you?"

Juliana. Her name was as beautiful as she was.

Webster stared up at her, knowing immediately why she had finally told him her name. He had let her help him, let her see him sick and weak. She was invading what was very private and personal. In return, she was infringing on her own privacy, making them, in some sense, even.

"Juliana," he whispered, trying her name out.

This time she was the one who couldn't meet his eyes, as if the sound of her name on his lips somehow embarrassed her.

"You have to promise to call me that only when we're alone," she said softly, "not when other guests are around."

Only when we're alone, thought Webster, savoring the sound of those words. He nodded.

She stood up then, and he closed his eyes, slipping into a feverish dream. Juliana was there, on her Harley, and she was laughing. The sound of her laughter sent chills of pleasure up and down his spine.

"Come on, Web," she said. "We have to get you into the bathtub."

"I don't take baths," Web said. "I take showers."

"Well, today you're going to take a bath."

She had her arm around his waist, helping him walk into the bathroom. Her hands on his skin felt strong and cool, and his head felt as if he were floating. And sure enough, there in the bathroom, the big tub was filled with clean, clear water.

"Last time I took a bath I was about six," Web said. "I had a bunch of little boats."

"Come on, Webster."

"You got any boats?"

More laughter. "You could probably use your shampoo bottle," she said. "Just make sure the top's closed tightly, or else you'll have a bubble bath."

She still had her arms around him. He looked down at her, wishing he could kiss her, unable to remember why he couldn't. Oh, yeah, she didn't want him to. Last time he tried, she ran away. He wasn't going to risk that again. He closed his eyes as a wave of dizziness hit him. Oh yeah, he was sick, too. "I don't want to give you the flu," he said worriedly.

She smiled. "I had a flu shot. I'll be okay. Come on, I'll help you into the tub."

"With my underwear on?"

"You can take your shorts off if you want," she said.

"But, you're in the room."

"Yes, I'm in the room. I'm not going to let you get into the tub by yourself," she said firmly. "You'll slip and fall on your head. Keep 'em on if it bothers you."

Webster stared at the water. "Juliana," he said, drawing each syllable out, rolling her name off his tongue.

He looked down at her and smiled. His eyes held none of the crystal hardness, none of the ulterior motive that had always lurked beneath his smiles in the past. "I guess it's okay," he said, "as long as we're on a first-name basis."

But as he hooked his thumbs in the elastic waistband of his shorts, gravity interfered and he lost his balance. Juliana tried desperately to keep him upright, but he was simply too large. They fell onto the bathroom floor in a tangled pile of arms and legs.

Juliana stared up into Webster's face, only inches above her own. His dark blue eyes were slightly puzzled.

"This isn't a dream, is it?" he asked.

She shook her head, no.

A vast array of emotions flitted across his handsome face as he looked down at her. "I hope you appreciate the amount of restraint I'm using here," he said.

"I do," Juliana whispered, realizing suddenly that one of his big, muscular thighs was pressed up tightly between her legs. The heat radiating from him was incredible. Thank heavens for that, she thought. At least it hid the fire his nearness had started in her. "Please get off me, Web."

He rolled off her quickly, instantly apologetic. "I'm sorry," he said. "Maybe I should just leave my shorts on."

She caught his eye and smiled, a touch self-consciously. "Good idea," she said. "Let's get you into that tub. Carefully this time." Maybe if she sounded business-like, he wouldn't realize how rattled she was by his nearly naked body so close to hers. He was so tall, all hard muscles and tanned skin.

Webster sat down in the cool water with a groan. "You didn't tell me it would be freezing," he accused her.

"It's not freezing, it just feels that way to you because you're so hot."

"Big difference," Webster muttered.

"Slide down," she said, folding a towel to put under his head. "Lean back—you can rest your head on this."

He leaned his dark curls against the towel, looking up at her. "Thanks." Again, it was heartfelt. "When did you get your bike?"

"My Harley?" she asked.

He nodded.

"I've had that one for about three years. I got my first motorcycle about twelve years ago—when I was sixteen."

"That when you got that tattoo?"

"Yeah," she nodded. "I was . . . wild then."

"But you're not anymore?"

Juliana shook her head. "No. Being wild had a price."

"Like what?"

But she shook her head again, and didn't answer. "How do you feel?"

"Bad."

She sat on the edge of the tub and gently pushed his hair off his face. "I'm sorry," she said.

Webster closed his eyes, lulled by the gentle magic of her fingers. "I'm glad you're here," he said softly. "Juliana."

SEVEN

Webster woke up hungry. He hadn't felt anything but nausea for so long that at first, he didn't recognize the sensation. He opened his eyes slowly, but the headache was gone. His body still felt leaden, exhausted, and extremely weak. Even his fingers were weak; he couldn't've made a convincing fist if he wanted to.

He glanced at the clock. Seven-thirty A.M.

God, he was thirsty. There was an empty glass and a full bottle of cola on the bedside table. He pushed himself slowly up, dragging himself to the side of the bed so he could reach for the bottle.

"Web?" Juliana sat up, pushing her red-gold curls out of her face. "You okay?" she asked sleepily.

Webster stared at her in shock. She had been sleeping on the floor next to his bed.

She held up the basin. "You need this?"

He shook his head. "No."

She pulled herself to her feet, sitting next to him on the bed, as she reached out to feel his forehead. Cool. She closed her eyes in relief. And opened them as she felt Webster's warm fingers touch her face.

"You're so tired," he said, his voice gentle and full

of wonder. "You shouldn't have been sleeping on the floor."

She smiled at him then. "I didn't want to leave you alone. You were pretty sick for a while there."

"You stayed with me," he said, as if he couldn't quite believe it. "For how long?"

"Today's Friday," she said.

He'd gotten sick . . . when? He couldn't remember. "How many days?" he asked.

"It was only two nights."

Two nights . . . She'd stayed with him two whole nights. And the day in between, he remembered. Flashes of the past few days came to him, as if they were scenes from a movie.

Juliana reached for the glass, poured only an inch or so of cola into the bottom and handed it to him. He looked at the small ration of flat soda skeptically.

"Oh, come on," he said. "I feel much better. And I'm really thirsty."

"That's what you said last time," Juliana replied dryly.

In a flash, Webster remembered being thirsty, so thirsty, and drinking ginger ale. His stomach rejected it so quickly and absolutely that there wasn't any time for him to react. He'd gotten sick all over the bed. He groaned inwardly, remembering how patient Juliana had been, how she hadn't complained. She just changed the sheets and tucked him back into the bed.

"I'm sorry," he said softly, closing his eyes, letting the humiliation wash over him.

Juliana watched him for a moment. When he'd been so terribly sick, his fever had been so high he'd spent much of the time delirious or at least . . . silly. There had only been a few brief moments of lucidity when he seemed to realize his utter helplessness, when he knew just how intimately she was caring for him. At those times he was stricken with humility, the way he was right now.

This humble, subdued Webster Donovan was a far cry from the rude, arrogant man she'd met nearly an entire week ago. And she liked him much better. She hoped he'd stick around.

She leaned forward, kissing him lightly on the forehead. "It's okay," she said.

Web opened his eyes, shocked. She'd kissed him. She'd actually *kissed* him. True, it was the kind of kiss she might give to a puppy or an elderly great-uncle, but it was a kiss.

She stood up, moving toward the door. "I have guests arriving this evening," she said. "I have to do laundry and get the rooms ready."

She was wearing an old pair of gray sweat pants and a faded maroon Harvard sweat shirt. Her eyes still looked sleepy, and her hair was rumpled, but she smiled at him, and Webster thought he'd never seen her look better.

"I'll be back to check on you in about twenty minutes, okay?"

Webster nodded. "Did you go to Harvard?" he asked.

She looked at him blankly, until he motioned to her sweat shirt. She saw what she was wearing, and shook her head. "No," she said, and laughed.

Webster didn't get the joke, and she didn't explain.

Over the course of the day, Juliana came into his room often, bringing him minuscule amounts of saltine crackers and flat cola and ginger ale. She made sure he was covered up when he was asleep, and she brought him books and magazines when he was awake.

He really wanted her to sit and talk, but she didn't have time.

In the late afternoon, Juliana brought in a steaming bowl of chicken-and-rice soup, balanced on a bed tray.

"Zowie," Webster said, putting down the book he'd been reading. "Real food."

Juliana smiled, putting the tray down across his lap, trying to ignore the fact that the flannel shirt he wore was unbuttoned, exposing the hard muscles of his chest.

He hadn't shaved in days, and with the stubble on his face and his hair a nest of curls, he looked roguish and dangerous. But his smile softened the effect.

Webster watched as Juliana sat tiredly in the chair next to his bed. Her ratty sweats had disappeared, replaced by a quaint green-patterned Victorian dress. Gone were the loose curls around her face. Once again, she wore her hair primly back and up.

"I've got about an hour before the first guests are due to arrive," she said. "Heavens, I think this is the first time I've sat down all day."

He stirred the hot soup, letting some of the heat escape. "Maybe you should use the time to take a nap," he said.

Juliana sat up straight. "I'm sorry," she said. "You're probably working, reading at least. I should go, let you—"

"No!" The force of that one word startled even Webster. "I mean, please. I just thought you might want to rest. I guess I feel guilty for keeping you up two nights in a row."

"Don't worry," Juliana said, her lips twitching up into a bewitching smile. "I've figured out a way for you to repay me."

She could see the flash of interest in his dark-blue eyes. "Oh, really?"

"Yes, really. Maybe I'll tell you later this week."

"Not another secret?"

She smiled. "Eat your soup."

Webster took a spoonful of the fragrant broth, blowing gently on it before putting it in his mouth. "This tastes great," he murmured. "Thanks."

Juliana smiled her welcome, letting her eyes drift shut as he focused all of his attention and energy on eating the soup. After a while, the sound of the spoon hitting the bowl stopped, and she opened her eyes to find Webster watching her.

"You know," he said, "you can lie down over here." He motioned toward the other side of his big bed. "I don't bite."

"At least not too hard," Juliana said, repeating his own words. It seemed as if he'd said that to her years ago, but it had only been a few short days . . .

Webster saw wariness come into her eyes, as if she'd suddenly remembered who she was dealing with. She stood up tiredly, stretching her arms and back. "I better start baking for tomorrow's breakfast," she said, trying to sound casual, but really searching for a way to leave.

As he watched her walk toward the door, Webster was filled with sudden, gut-wrenching despair, far worse than any stomachache the flu had given him. Now that he was better, everything was going to go back to the way it had been. The easy familiarity between them would vanish, and Juliana would turn back into the cool, polite stranger.

Webster wasn't entirely sure what he wanted in his life, but he was dead certain that he didn't want *that* to happen.

"Juliana."

She turned and looked at him, her beautiful eyes guarded.

"Please . . ." he said. "Stay with me for a while." He held his breath then, waiting for her response.

She watched him steadily, her face expressionless.

"Talk to me," he said, quietly. "Please? I want— I'd *like* to know more about you."

Juliana saw naked honesty in his blue eyes. Honesty

and fear. Fear of what? Loneliness, maybe, she thought. Whatever it was, he wasn't being glib or smooth, and the end result was one hundred percent charm. Juliana walked back toward the bed and was rewarded by a flare of hopeful pleasure on his face. She leaned against the footboard.

"Over the past two and a half days," she said, a glint of amusement in her eyes, "you've done nothing but question me about where I grew up, how long I've lived here in Benton, how long I've had my horse— that is, when you weren't, shall I say, otherwise engaged . . . ?"

He laughed. "No fair. Now you're *trying* to embarrass me."

"Do you always ask so many questions?"

"I used to be a reporter," he said. "It's in my blood."

He was quiet for a moment, looking down at the floral pattern of the bedspread. "You know, either I don't remember, or you didn't answer my questions."

"I answered some of 'em," she said with a smile. She crossed to the chair and sat down, pulling her feet up on the seat, tucking them under her long skirt, resting her chin in her hand as she looked at him. "Let's see, you asked me how old I was. I'm almost twenty-eight. You asked how old I was when I had my first kiss, and who the lucky guy was, and I said fourteen and Emilio Cardonza. You asked me where I was born, and I said Springfield. You asked if I had any brothers or sisters, and I said no. You asked me a million questions about where I went to college and what my major was. I didn't answer them. I also didn't answer when you asked me how old I was when I lost my virginity."

Webster groaned. "I didn't really ask you that, did I?"

"You did. How old are *you*?"

"Thirty-four."

"Where were *you* born?" she asked.

"Ocala, Florida," Webster said. "My parents owned a ranch. We raised thoroughbreds and some not-so-thoroughbreds. Good horses, though."

"You must've had a great childhood," Juliana said, envy in her voice.

"Too many people assume that," he said.

She looked at him, her eyebrow raised. "You didn't?"

"My parents didn't win any prizes." He shrugged. "And my childhood pretty much ended when they sent me to boarding school. I was only home in the summers."

"Still, even to spend your summers on a ranch, with all those horses . . ." Juliana said. "You must be an excellent rider."

"I am."

She smiled. "Careful—don't be a jerk. The correct response is to smile modestly and say, 'I'm not bad.' "

Webster grinned, not at all modestly. "But I'm not 'not bad.' I'm excellent."

"Maybe one of these days, when you're feeling better," Juliana said, "we can go out riding, and you can prove it."

"I'd like that," he said. "I don't get to ride much these days. There aren't too many stables in downtown Boston."

"Is that where you live?"

He nodded. "I have an apartment on Boylston Street."

"I lived in Boston for a few years," Juliana said. "Brookline, really. I was seventeen. It was when I first went to live with Alicia."

"Alicia?" Web asked.

"My great-aunt," she said. "You spoke to her on the phone, remember?"

Webster shifted his weight, trying to get comfortable.

"Yeah, I remember. Is she really your great-aunt? She sounded so young."

"She is young. She's only seventy-eight," Juliana said.

"Only seventy-eight . . ."

"She'll be back in a few days," she said. "She's spending a couple of weeks on St. Thomas, visiting an old friend. She likes to travel. She lived in Africa for years. She took me there once. We went on a safari."

"You mean . . . *hunting*?"

"No guns, only cameras," Juliana said. "It was wonderful. Alicia is an amazing woman."

Webster pulled one of the pillows out behind him, lying flat on his back. Maybe that would help. "So why did you live with her when you were a teenager? Were you going to college in Boston?"

He turned on his side to look at her, grimacing as his back twinged.

"Do you want me to rub your back?" Juliana asked suddenly.

Webster smiled ruefully. "Yeah, I'd love it. But do you really want to, or are you just trying to avoid answering my questions?"

She rose gracefully from the chair and crossed to the bed. Nudging his hips with the back of her hand, she said, "Roll over."

Webster rolled onto his stomach, shrugging out of his loose shirt. He pulled a pillow up under his arms and rested his chin on his hands, then closed his eyes as her strong, cool fingers began to massage the tight muscles in his shoulders. This was the stuff fantasies were made of.

Juliana moved her hands down his broad, strong back. His skin was sleek and warm and so smooth beneath her fingers. She liked touching him. She had wanted to touch him from the moment she woke up this morning. But that was nothing new. She'd wanted to touch him from the first moment she set eyes on him.

The big surprise was realizing that she liked Webster Donovan. She really liked him. Maybe *too* much.

But he was rich. He'd grown up the rich son of rich parents, just like Dennis. And just like Dennis, he would condemn her when he found out.

She might as well tell Webster the whole story, she thought. She *had* to tell him in order to stop wondering what he would think if he knew. She *should* tell him now before she really, truly cared what he thought.

"You asked me why I went to live with Alicia," she said, her voice low. "It wasn't because of college. I didn't go to college. I didn't even finish high school."

Webster heard her pause and realized that she wanted him to say something. "This feels really great," he murmured. "Please don't stop."

It wasn't what she expected him to say. There was another long pause. Then she asked, "Aren't you shocked?"

Webster didn't answer right away, and when he did, he spoke carefully, as if he were considering each word he said. "I don't shock easily," he said. "So what if you didn't finish high school? It's a shame, but only because you didn't get a chance to experience college life. You certainly seem well-educated. In fact, you're probably better read than most college grads."

Juliana was silent, her hands traveling back up toward his neck. She slipped her fingers under his soft, dark curls, feeling him relax underneath her, wishing that she could get rid of her own tension as easily. She had to tell him the rest.

She spoke again, her voice still low, but clear. "I lived with Alicia because . . . she was my only relative who wanted custody of me after I got out of reform school."

It was said so matter-of-factly that Webster had to

replay her words in his mind at least twice before he understood what she had said.

Reform school. After she got out of . . . reform school!

He rolled over, looking up at her. "Congratulations," he said, pulling himself into a sitting position. "You've shocked me. Why were you in reform school? For how long? When? How old were you?"

She folded her hands carefully in her lap. "I was sixteen. When I was charged with breaking and entering and grand theft, larceny, I came really close to being tried as an adult. But I was a first-time offender. I'd run away so many times the judge didn't want to send me back home, so . . ." She shrugged. "If Alicia hadn't petitioned for custody, I would've ended up inside until my eighteenth birthday. As it was, the five months I spent in there was way too long."

Juliana risked looking up at Webster. He was watching her steadily, but his eyes held no accusations, no revulsion, no pity—only warmth. "It must've been awful," he said.

"It scared me to death," she admitted. "Being locked up like that, constantly watched . . ."

"Were you guilty?"

She nodded, yes, unable to speak the word. "I was living on my own, in the street. I had two options when it came to surviving, besides going back home, that is. I chose stealing." She looked at him, waiting.

Webster just watched her. He didn't say anything.

"Well?" she finally asked.

"Well what?"

"This is where you're supposed to say something clever to get me out of the room so you can count the money in your wallet, make sure it's all there," Juliana said.

Webster laughed, then stopped as he realized she

wasn't kidding. "Oh, come on. When was the last time you stole something?" he asked.

"It was only that one time," she said, "and that was only because I was so hungry."

"When you were sixteen," Webster said. "Twelve years ago. God almighty, Juliana, I hope you don't intend to judge *me* by the mistakes *I* made twelve years ago."

Juliana looked down at her hands, willing away the tears that had somehow leapt into her eyes. "No," she said softly. "I'd never do that."

"I also hope that you don't judge me by the mistakes I made just last week," Webster said softly.

She looked up at him, startled, remembering the man she'd first known as Webster Donovan.

His eyes held none of the crystal hardness she'd seen in that other Webster. Instead they held such sensitivity and warmth she felt she had a glimpse of this man's soul.

"I won't," she said, then managed to smile. "You know, Webster Donovan, I think we just might be able to be friends."

He smiled back at her. "Friends would be a really good place to start."

EIGHT

The next few days passed quickly, and Webster finally felt well enough to venture downstairs. The first day he was up and about, he followed Juliana into the kitchen after breakfast, staying and chatting as she cleaned up the dishes. The second day, he grabbed a sponge and helped. The third day, he followed her up to the guest rooms, continuing a running dialog on his favorite books, authors, movies, and musical groups, peppered with endless questions about her own favorites.

As they went into the second room, and he started to help her strip the bed, she had to laugh. "Webster, I've never seen anyone procrastinate as diligently as you."

He looked across the bed at her, smiling slightly. "I'm not procrastinating," he said.

"You're not writing," she pointed out.

"Yeah, but I'm not procrastinating."

She motioned to him, standing there, a pillowcase in his hands. "If this isn't procrastination, what is it?"

"It's just . . . well . . ." He cleared his throat, tossing the pillowcases into the laundry basket. When he looked back at her, the softness in his eyes nearly took her breath away. "I just want to be with you, Juliana," he said.

She had to turn away, unsure of what to say and equally unsure how to feel. *Light,* she thought desperately. *Keep it light.* "Good," she said. "Then today you can start paying me back for all those days I waited on you hand and foot."

He leaned on the bed, eyebrows on the rise. "You want me to wait on *you* hand and foot?"

She threw a pillow at his head. He caught it and began stuffing it into a clean pillowcase. "I've got five ladies arriving at four-thirty," she said. "They'll be here for dinner tonight and tomorrow. If you're game, I'd like you to help me entertain them."

Web's eyebrows rose even higher. "Entertain? You mean, like tap dance? Recite poetry?"

"The poetry would be nice." Juliana smiled. "Look, I'll show you what I mean. Come with me."

Intrigued, Webster followed her out of the room and down the hall. "Curiouser and curiouser," he murmured as she led the way up the stairs to the third floor.

He watched silently as she took a key from a long chain that she wore around her neck and unlocked the deadbolt to her apartment. Her long skirt swept after her as she went through the doorway. Webster stood outside, not sure if he should follow.

After a moment she came back to the door. "What are you waiting for?" she asked.

"An invitation, I think," he said. "You told me so absolutely that your apartment was off limits my feet refuse to step over the threshold."

Juliana made a face at him. "That was back when you were a jerk," she said. "But all right, I'll humor you. Won't you come in, Mr. Donovan?"

"Thank you, Miss Anderson," he said, stepping into

the room. "You know, *I* haven't changed. It's your perception of me that's been altered.

"What are you saying? That you're still a jerk?"

"Nice place," he said in admiration, looking around the spacious room. "You've made yourself your own little Greenwich Village loft here, way the hell out in the middle of nowhere. It's so modern I'm shocked."

"I thought you weren't easily shocked," Juliana said with a smile.

"I'm not." Webster crossed the room to get a better look at her exercise gear. "Oh, wow, look what you've got! Your own private health club. Could I—? Sorry." He shook his head, as if amazed at his audacity.

"Use my equipment sometime?" Juliana asked, finishing the sentence for him, with a smile. "Why don't I dangle that over your head as additional incentive for helping me out tonight and tomorrow?"

"Absolutely. Good incentive. I love what you've done with the skylights," Webster said, his eyes following the line of the ceiling. "How many houseplants do you have? Is it four or five hundred?"

"Not that many." Juliana laughed.

"Aren't you afraid you'll hyperventilate from all the extra oxygen these monsters give off?"

"Watch what you call them. They're listening!"

"Oh my God," Webster said, drawn to another part of the room. "You hypocrite! Your brochure clearly boasts that there are no TVs in your bed and breakfast, but that's got to be the biggest television I've ever seen in my life! I'm crushed! All this time, I pictured you sitting around doing needlepoint in the evening, when really you were up here watching *Funniest Home Videos*, and *Ren and Stimpy*."

"Webster, what do I have to do to get your attention?" Juliana said.

"You've probably got a microwave somewhere around here, too, don't you?"

"Webster, get over here and take your clothes off!"

She could see the shock in his blue eyes clear across the room. "Okay," he said. "That got my attention."

"I have something I want you to try on," she said calmly, opening her closet door and disappearing inside. When she came back out, he was standing by the end of her platform bed. He turned to look at her.

The clothes Juliana held were covered with a thin plastic from the dry cleaners. She pulled it up to reveal a gentleman's black Victorian evening coat, complete with tails, a vest, a black pair of trousers, and a frilled white shirt.

Webster laughed. "Where did you get that?"

"I have a costume chest." She smiled. "I remembered there was a suit that no one could ever wear because it was much too big. I almost threw it out last year. Lucky for you, I didn't. I sent it out to have it cleaned a few days ago."

"Lucky for me," he echoed. He sat down on her bed, pulling off his boots.

"You can change in the bathroom if you want," she said, but he had already stepped out of his jeans. "Or not," she added weakly.

It hadn't even been a week since she'd taken care of him, since she'd seen him with less on than the red shorts he was wearing now. But he'd been barely mobile, hardly even conscious. The effect was quite a bit different than seeing him upright and in motion, muscles rippling, as he pulled on the pair of black trousers. If he noticed her staring, he kindly didn't comment.

"I get it," he said. "You want me to wear this down to dinner, right? Be part of the Victorian scenery?"

"I think you can probably manage to be more than mere scenery," she said.

He fastened the pants easily, then pulled on the shirt. "What the heck . . . ?" he said, holding up his arms. The sleeves seemed to be much too long.

"Cuffs," Juliana realized. "You'll need cuff links."

She went back into her closet and came out pulling a trunk behind her. A man's jewelry box was close to the top, and she took it out, rummaging through it until she came up with several shiny gold cuff links.

"Better let me do this," she said, and he held out his arm. Their eyes met as she touched him, and she quickly looked down. They were standing much too close for her to gaze into his eyes for any length of time, she thought. If she did, he might realize that she wanted him to kiss her. Her fingers fumbled and she dropped a cuff link on the floor.

Sweet heavens, she thought, as she picked it up. She did, she really did. She wanted Webster to kiss her.

She fastened the metal links through the button holes in the cuff of one sleeve and then the other, realizing that she was exerting an awful lot of energy to dress a man she'd much rather be undressing.

Glancing up, she found Webster's eyes on her face. She couldn't hold back a nervous laugh.

"What's the joke?" he said, his eyes so sweetly uncertain.

Juliana didn't answer.

Webster watched her closely for a moment. Her cheeks were slightly flushed, and she wouldn't meet his eyes. He was dying to kiss her, to pull her back with him on top of her big bed, and make love to her with the sunlight streaming in through the skylight, warming their skin. But for now, she wanted only to be friends, he reminded himself. He was going to take this slowly; it mattered too much to him to rush it.

Juliana risked a glance at Webster. He was having trouble getting the evening coat off the dry cleaner's hanger. She moved close to him, unfastening the hidden pins that the cleaner used to keep the garment secured. Webster didn't take a step backward, and when she looked at him, their faces were only inches apart.

This is it, thought Juliana. He was going to kiss her now.

This is it, thought Webster. She was testing him. But uh-uh, no way. He wasn't going to risk being a jerk again. But not kissing her took effort. His hands shook slightly as he tried to button the evening coat. And if Juliana noticed, she didn't say a word.

"How do I look?" Webster struck a pose.

The moment was gone. Juliana might have been disappointed if she hadn't seen his fingers fumble the buttons of his coat. He was just as rattled as she was, she thought, maybe even more so.

"Come see." Juliana led the way into her bathroom, turning on the lights.

The bathroom was all black-and-white tile, with a floor-to-ceiling mirror on one wall. A huge Jacuzzi sat under a skylight, surrounded by—what else, Webster thought—more plants. There was a shower stall off to one side, a double row of sinks with another big mirror above it. The entire room was about the size of his bedroom downstairs. "Very impressive," he said.

"Yes, you do look good," Juliana said.

The trim black trousers were probably a little too snug across the seat of his pants, but the jacket fit as if it had been made for him. With his dark curls, he looked as if he'd stepped out from a time machine. They both did, Juliana realized, although Webster was dressed more formally than she was.

"I was talking about the room, but now that you mention it, I look—" Webster gave her a sideways glance and a small smile. "—not bad."

Juliana laughed. "Oh, Webster, you learn so quickly. But the big question is," she said, leaning back against the wall and crossing her arms, "can you stay in character?"

* * *

Juliana stood gracefully, moving to the dining room sideboard and picking up the heavy coffee pot. "More coffee, Mr. Donovan," she murmured as she passed his chair.

"No thank you, Miss Anderson," he replied. "I've had enough."

"Perhaps I might ask you to escort the ladies into the front parlor, while I clear the table?" she said.

"Of course," he said. His smile was serene, but his eyes told her that she had the easier job.

By the time she made her way into the parlor, Webster had set up a card table, and he and the ladies were playing cards. They quickly made room for Juliana at the table, and she sat down. Her eyebrow rose when Webster told her they were playing poker. Poker? But the ladies seemed eager and willing.

"All right, ladies—" Webster looked around the table, his eyes lingering on Juliana "—the game is night baseball, in the rain. . . ."

It was after eleven before the last of the guests said good night.

"They like you," Juliana said, watching Webster put away the card table as she poured them each a snifter of brandy.

He waited until he heard the doors close tightly on the second floor before he said, "Maybe too much. I'm locking my door tonight. Before dinner, one of those ladies pinched me on the cheek, and I'm not talking about my face."

Juliana handed him his glass, trying hard not to laugh.

"It's not funny," he said indignantly.

"Webster," she said. "I didn't tell you this before, but . . . those ladies are nuns."

"No!"

"Yes. They're from a convent in Worcester."

"I swear to God," he said, "appropriately enough,

I suppose, but I swear, *somebody* definitely pinched me. God, a *nun*! Who would've thought."

"A nun didn't pinch you." Juliana carried her own glass over to the fire and swirled it in her hand, smiling up at Webster.

"I'm telling you, Juliana—"

"*I* did."

He stared at her. "You . . . ?"

She nodded, trying hard not to laugh.

"All that talk about staying in character," he said, "and *you* go and . . . I'm shocked."

He started to laugh.

"Liz called today," Juliana said. "She and Sam are throwing a party this coming Monday night. I don't have any other guests scheduled to come in that night, so I told her I'd be there. Would you like to go?"

Webster stopped laughing. He set his glass of brandy down very carefully on the mantle and turned to look at Juliana. She stood several feet away from him, the firelight playing off her beautiful face. But her eyes sparkled with a light of their own as she smiled at him.

"Are you . . " he started, then stopped. "You're not . . ."

One delicate eyebrow rose, waiting for him to go on.

"With you?" he finally asked.

"Yes." She took a sip of her brandy.

"You mean, kind of like . . . a date?"

"I mean exactly like a date."

Webster nodded, then laughed, then nodded again. He looked back at her, and his eyes were the deepest blue she'd ever seen. "I'd love to go on a date with you," he said, his voice soft, but very, very certain.

Juliana's pulse raced. She liked Webster as a friend. She was comfortable with him as her friend. But there was something that was more than friendship between them. There was something that boiled turbulently, just below the surface every time she got close to him, every time they accidentally touched.

Webster picked up his brandy and swirled it around the glass, staring into the dark liquid. "Is this the kind of date where, after it's over, I can kiss you good night?" he asked. He was trying to be light, trying to sound like he was teasing, but Juliana knew that he wasn't. His eyes were dead serious when he looked back at her.

She took a step toward him. "We don't need to go on a date to kiss each other good night," she said.

He swallowed, his eyes moving down to her mouth for a moment. He put his glass back on the mantle and shook his head again. "Juliana . . ." He said her name softly, taking his time with it. "I wouldn't want to be accused of being a jerk."

"If you don't kiss me good night, Webster, you will be a jerk," she said with a smile.

He moved toward her, and she put her own glass up on the mantle. But he stopped just short of taking her into his arms. Their eyes locked, and Webster felt his heart pound. It was so loud she had to be able to hear it.

"Juliana, I'm scared to death," he said softly. "I'm afraid of doing this wrong, of saying something stupid. And at the same time, I'm afraid that I'm too scared of blowing it to be able to do it right."

She smiled at him again. "I guess, then, it can wait another day or so," she said, turning toward the door.

But he caught her arm, pulling her back to him. "No, it can't," he said hoarsely.

Juliana caught her breath as she felt his arms around her. With one hand, he touched her face, brushing her hair back as his eyes caressed her.

Slowly, so slowly and gently, his lips met hers. Juliana felt herself melt against him and slipped her arms up around his neck.

He'd kissed her before, but back then they'd been strangers. Then the kiss had been driven by pure passion, by basic physical need. Now the passion was still there—Juliana felt it in the way he held her, in his arms, in his body—but there was also a sweetness that came from their friendship, from shared secrets and laughter.

She opened her mouth to him, but felt him hesitate. He was still afraid of stepping out of line. But when she touched his lips lightly with her tongue, his arms tightened around her and he hesitated no longer. She could hear him groan, way back deep in his throat as his tongue swept into her mouth. She pressed herself against him, matching the fierceness of his kisses, wanting him as much as he wanted her.

"God, Juliana," he breathed, still holding her close, her head against his shoulder. She could feel his heart racing, hear his unsteady breathing.

She lifted her face to him, and he kissed her again and again—deep, soft, sweet kisses that left her trembling and wanting more.

But more would have to wait.

She pulled back only slightly, but he immediately released her. "Good night, Web," she whispered. "Sleep well." And she went up the stairs, her skirts rustling quietly.

Webster stared into the dying embers of the fire, unable to keep a smile from his face. Sleep well? Highly unlikely. He'd be lucky if he got to sleep at all.

NINE

Juliana locked her apartment door behind her. She tucked the key carefully into the high neck of her blouse, then tiptoed down the stairs past the guest bedrooms. It was so early the sun hadn't even come up yet, but rising at this time was the price she had to pay for not washing up the dishes after dinner.

She smiled, thinking of the way Webster had kissed her last night. It hadn't been easy to fall asleep, thinking of him just one floor below her, yet somehow she felt rested and refreshed.

She pushed open the door to the kitchen, thinking, darn, she'd left the light on all night, then stopped and stared.

Webster stared back at her from where he was standing at the sink, elbow deep in dishwater. He smiled, then checked the kitchen clock. "Good morning."

Juliana looked around the kitchen in amazement. It was spotless—all the dishes and pots washed, all the counters wiped and shining.

He rinsed the last of the pot lids, balancing it on an already precariously tall pile in the dish rack, and let the sudsy water out of the sink. It vanished with a slurp down the drain as Webster wiped his hands on a dish towel.

He was wearing his ratty gray sweat pants and a loose tank top that barely covered his muscular upper body. His feet were bare and his hair was wild, as usual. Sweet heavens, he looked good enough to eat.

Juliana sniffed the air. Was that . . . coffee?

Webster crossed to the coffee maker and poured out a mug, presenting it to her with a flourish, handle out.

"Web, what's going on?" Juliana asked. "It must've taken you hours to—"

"One hour and twenty-two minutes." He grinned.

She looked at the clock. The digital readout flashed 5:25. If he'd been up at *four* o'clock, then he'd surely been up at *three* o'clock. And if he'd been up at *three* o'clock, then he surely hadn't gone to bed at all.

"I'm celebrating!" he proclaimed, throwing his arms open wide.

Juliana lifted one delicate eyebrow. "You're celebrating. So naturally, you clean my kitchen . . . ?"

He shrugged. "It seemed like a good way to pass the time until you woke up."

She put down her coffee mug and took a dry dish towel from the back of the pantry door. "Thank you," she said, smiling. "But aren't you planning to sleep at all today?"

He grabbed a second dish towel and began helping her dry the dishes. "I'll take a nap after breakfast," he said.

"Promise?" she asked.

"Well . . ."

"I don't want you to get sick again," she said sternly. "Promise you'll take a nap, and I'll let you use my workout gear later this afternoon."

"Deal." He grinned. "Hey, aren't you going to ask me why I'm celebrating?"

Juliana hung the pots from the rack above the stove,

stopping to turn on the oven, preheating it for the coffee cake she planned to make for breakfast. "Okay, tell me. Why are you celebrating?"

"Last night, after being tremendously inspired—" he waggled his eyebrows at Juliana "—I went up to my room and wrote an entire outline for my book."

"Webster, that's great news!" Juliana said.

"Yeah, I thought so, too," he said, helping her carry the ingredients for the coffee cake to the table. "Now I can start writing."

Juliana was measuring cupfuls of rich, whole-wheat flour, and she looked up, giving him a sideways glance, unsuccessfully trying to hide a smile. "Does this mean you're going to stop following me around in the mornings?"

"Do you want me to stop following you around in the mornings?"

Juliana handed him the heavy flour canister, and he put it away in the cupboard, looking back at her expectantly, waiting for her answer.

She carefully measured out the baking powder and salt, adding it to the flour before she said, "How can I answer that, knowing every minute you spend down here in the kitchen with me, you're *not* writing your next literary masterpiece?"

"I guess you really don't have to answer," Webster said, crossing the kitchen to stand beside her, "because I fully intend to keep following you around. And not just in the mornings." He reached out and brushed a stray red-gold curl from her face.

She looked up at him. His eyes were soft and very dark blue—exactly the way they'd looked last night before he'd kissed her.

"Just so you know," Juliana said, her voice suddenly husky, "I also found last night tremendously inspiring."

Webster leaned forward then and kissed her. It was

little more than a gentle caress, his lips brushing lightly against hers, but it was perfect—undemanding and sincere. Juliana found herself holding on to the edge of the table.

"So," Web said, consciously making an effort to break the mood. He looked from the array of ingredients still out on the table to the big mixing bowl. "What goes in there next? Where's your cookbook?"

"Sugar," Juliana said faintly. "And I don't use a cookbook."

"You don't use a . . . how can you make food taste so wonderful without using a cookbook?" Webster said, reeling across the kitchen. "I'm shocked! Again!"

Juliana laughed, regaining her equilibrium now that he wasn't standing quite so close to her. "Believe me, I've probably made this particular coffee cake four hundred times." She tapped her head. "I've got the recipe up here. Permanently."

"What do you want me to do then? Start dueling with the fresh fruit?"

Juliana motioned to the cutlery in the wood block. "Choose your weapon," she said.

Webster selected a viciously sharp-looking knife and happily went to work cutting a huge pile of fresh fruit into bite-sized pieces.

As they worked, Webster kept up his usual steady stream of conversation, telling Juliana about the day he decided to take his father's prize mare for a ride—only days before the very pregnant horse was due to foal. "I didn't know why the horse was so damn fat," he said. "I thought she needed the exercise. I was only six years old. I mean, I knew about sex—we ran a stud service, for crying out loud. But people would bring their mares to our farm, our stallions would service them, and then they'd leave. This was the first time I'd been around anything even remotely pregnant. Man, you should've seen my father's face when he saw me riding that mare bareback around the corral. . . ." He laughed, shaking his head.

"Did you get punished?" Juliana asked.

Webster was silent for a moment. The sound of his knife hitting the cutting board with solid *thwacks* was the only noise in the kitchen.

"Yeah," he finally said.

But he didn't say anything else. Juliana looked over at him. He was pretending to be engrossed in cutting a pear.

"What happened?" she asked.

"My father gave me the cold, silent treatment for an entire week. Then . . . he shipped me off to boarding school." Webster was trying to be casual, blasé even, but Juliana could see an echo of the little boy he'd once been in his eyes. And that little boy was still indignant, outraged, and deeply, deeply hurt.

Juliana thought about Liz and Sam's son, Chris, who had just turned nine. She couldn't imagine sending a child even *that* young away from home. And *six*! A six-year-old was hardly more than a baby.

"I'm sorry," she said.

"Yeah, well, you know, life goes on," he said, scraping the fruit on his cutting board into the big plastic container.

"I do know," she said quietly, and when he looked up at her, he knew she understood.

Webster stood at the counter, mixing the batter for pancakes.

"What's next?" he asked.

"Eggs. Three," she said, carrying the heavy plates and silverware into the living room. The door swung softly shut behind her.

"Three eggs," Webster repeated, opening the refrigerator. A huge carton of fresh eggs was on the bottom shelf. He pulled three eggs from the box and began juggling them clumsily as he turned to cross the kitchen floor.

Except the kitchen floor was occupied by a small, elderly lady in a long, black coat and matching hat.

Webster grabbed at two of the eggs and fumbled the third, catching it just before it hit the ground.

"Nice save," the lady said, one eyebrow slightly raised.

Her rather regal gaze swept up and down Webster, and he became acutely aware of the hole in the knee of his sweat pants. He put the eggs on the counter and ran his hands through his hair in a useless attempt to make it less dishevelled.

"Can I help you?" he asked.

"Who the heck are you?" she asked him.

"Webster Donovan."

She nodded, her piercing gray eyes settling on his face.

"I just finished reading your book," she said. "You're a fine writer—good style, smooth delivery, a sincere, personal voice. I enjoyed it immensely."

"Well, thanks," Webster said. "I'm glad, but—"

"How's the second novel coming?" she asked. She put her purse on the kitchen table and began taking off her coat, still watching him closely.

She saw the flash of passion spark in the young man's eyes, as his handsome face broke into a slow grin. "I wrote the outline last night," he said. "Finally."

"Aha," she said, pulling her hatpins out, and taking the tiny black hat off her thick gray curls. "Broke out of your writer's block, did you? Good for you."

Webster stared at her. Underneath her coat, she wore dark blue sweat pants and a white blouse under a knitted red vest. She had a pair of running shoes on her tiny feet, with pom-poms at the ends of her laces. Her face was beautiful, the lines and wrinkles adding dignity and wisdom to her countenance. She could have been anywhere from sixty to one hundred years old. But she moved with the vitality and youthfulness of a young girl.

"Excuse me for not knowing, but . . . who the heck are *you*?" Webster asked, echoing her words to him.

She laughed—a quick burst of sound. "I'm Alicia Dupree," she said. "Is my niece around here somewhere?"

"Juliana's getting the dining room ready," he said, breaking the eggs into the mixing bowl.

Alicia gave Webster another long, appraising look, thinking, Juliana, huh? In the five years they'd run this guest house, Jule hadn't allowed anyone to become familiar enough with her to call her by her first name. And since when did a guest work in the kitchen?

The door to the dining room swung open, and Juliana came into the room. Alicia watched Webster smile at her niece and saw his eyes light with the same passion she'd seen when he talked about his novel. *He's in love with her*, she thought. She *knew* just from talking to him on the phone that the two young folks would hit it off. But, oh dear, maybe coming back early was a mistake.

Alicia turned to her niece, hoping to see the same light in her eyes as Juliana looked at the young man, but Jule had already spotted her, and was coming toward her for a welcome-home hug.

"You're back early," Juliana said, her face showing nothing but pleasure at seeing her great-aunt.

"How's business?" Alicia asked.

"As usual for this time of year." Juliana smiled. "Heavy on the weekends, light during the week."

"Any word from our mysterious reviewer?"

Juliana shook her head. "I don't know, Al. We had an awful lot of return guests— Oh, the Edgewoods were here. They said to say hello. There were one or two first-timers, but nobody really looked like a reviewer.''

"Reviewer?" Webster asked, frowning slightly.

Alicia poured herself a cup of coffee, stirring in some milk. "Once every two years, the *Boston Globe* does a big spread on bed and breakfasts in western Massachusetts. Usually they send a letter telling who's coming and when they'll arrive. We haven't heard anything from them this year, so maybe they're doing it differently. I always did think it was foolish of them to tip their hand that way. *Of course* a guest house is going to get out its best silver and polish everything up real pretty if they know a reviewer is coming. It's the sneak attack that gets an effective review.''

Juliana smiled at her aunt. "I like being warned. I like knowing when it's going to happen.''

Alicia laughed. "You like being sure that you'll make your special raisin bread for the morning the reviewer's here. You're just as bad as the rest of 'em.''

"It's true,'' Juliana said, her smile suddenly cheeky. "A review can make or break a bed and breakfast. I'd do just about *anything* for a good one.''

Alicia looked up to find Webster's eyes on Juliana, a soft look on his face. He probably hadn't heard a single word they'd said, she realized, laughing to herself.

She looked at her niece, but Jule's face was carefully devoid of emotion as she met Webster's eyes. The young woman turned and serenely finished mixing the pancake batter.

"I'll cook dinner tonight," Alicia said suddenly.

"Alicia, you don't have to—"

"No, I've made up my mind. All you have to do is show up at seven o'clock with an appetite,'' the older woman said firmly. "You can take the afternoon off, go ride that horse of yours.'' *And take this young man with you,* she added silently.

"May I come along?" Webster asked Juliana softly.
Attaboy! Alicia silently cheered him on.

"I thought you wanted to use my exercise bike," she said.

"I'd rather go riding," he said. "With you."

Alicia smiled to herself. She liked this fellow. He didn't pull his punches. She felt Juliana glance at her, and she busied herself folding the cloth napkins that were out on the kitchen table.

"All right," Juliana said. "We'll leave at three-thirty. But that means you've got to go upstairs and go to sleep—right now."

"Deal," he said.

Out of the corner of her eye, Alicia saw him touch Juliana's face lightly with his fingers before he left the room. "See you at three-thirty," he said. "Nice meeting you, Alicia."

"Same here," she called back.

Alicia waited until the blush had left her niece's cheeks.

"Nice young man," she said.

"Uh-huh," Juliana agreed, heating the pancake griddle.

"Seems to like you an awful lot."

Juliana didn't respond.

"He's nothing at all like Dennis," Alicia said, trying to get any kind of reaction from the younger woman.

"Thank goodness for *that*," Juliana muttered.

"I taped Mr. Donovan's book for you while I was on vacation," Alicia said.

"You *did*?" Juliana looked up, her eyes sparkling with pleasure. "Liz lent me her copy. I've been dying to read it—"

"It just came out in paperback," Alicia said. "I saw it in the airport as I was waiting for my plane. Picked it up, couldn't put it down."

"Is it really that good?"

"You'll see."

"Thanks, Alicia," Juliana said quietly.

"Uh-huh."

The air was crisp, the cold more biting than it should be for a late-October afternoon. Clouds hung heavily in the sky, dark gray and threatening.

Captain snorted, his warm breath white in the chill air. Juliana looked at Webster, who was riding Sam Beckwith's horse, Firebrand, as if he had been born in the saddle. He practically had, she reminded herself.

He smiled at her, that familiar, lazy grin that could start a fire deep inside her.

She wanted him to kiss her the way he had last night. She wanted to feel his arms around her. She wanted to run her fingers through his gleaming hair . . . Which right now was mostly hidden under a beat-up old cowboy hat he'd pulled out of the trunk of his car when they'd arrived at the stables.

With that hat, his jeans and boots, and his soft, brown calfskin jacket, he looked like a cowboy. He looked like a man able to take on any physical hardship or difficulty that came his way, a rugged outdoorsman. He didn't look like the kind of man who could write words sensitive and poignant enough to bring tears to her eyes.

"I read your book today," she said. She'd gone up to her room right after breakfast and listened to the tapes Alicia had made for her. She hadn't stopped listening even for lunch.

His expression changed, and uncertainty crept into his eyes. "Oh," he said. He squinted out over the length of the pasture, reining in Firebrand.

Juliana halted Captain next to him. "It was . . . not bad."

He glanced at her and saw the teasing smile twitching at the corners of her mouth.

"I loved it," she admitted. "You know, the way you write is so natural. It's so much like the way you talk. I'd really love it if . . ." Her voice trailed off.

"What?" he asked.

She looked away from him, embarrassed.

"What?" he asked again. The warm curiosity in his eyes made her realize he wouldn't simply let it go.

"Someday, could you . . . read it to me?" she asked, adding softly, "I mean, not while you're so busy, trying to write this other book, but—"

He reached over, picked up her hand, and kissed her wrist on the spot between her glove and her jacket sleeve. Juliana felt a shiver go up her spine. Captain sidled, though, and Webster let go of her hand.

"I'd love to," he said, his voice husky as he suddenly imagined himself lying in a warm bed with Juliana. His arm would be around her, and her head would rest against his chest. Her beautiful eyes would be closed, and he would feel her breath warm against his skin as she breathed. And he would read out loud to her from his own book. . . .

He grinned to himself. The way she had asked, she'd implied it would be an imposition, as if he wouldn't be thrilled to read his own words to the woman that he—

He broke off his thought, suddenly terribly confused.

Juliana was stroking Captain's neck, and when she felt his eyes on her, she looked up and smiled.

The woman that he loved, thought Webster, suddenly unable to breathe. Except he didn't believe in love. It didn't exist.

You're just mixed up, he tried to tell himself. *You've mistaken simple desire for something else*.

And he did desire her. That was clear. God almighty, just look at her sitting astride that horse, he thought.

Captain was eager to run, and he broke away. Juliana skillfully brought the animal back under control, and as

Webster watched, the muscles in her thighs tightened underneath her jeans as she urged the horse back toward him. He wanted her long, strong legs around him like that. Damn, just thinking about it made him hard.

Yeah, he didn't really love her. It was just his desire for her making him a little crazy. Wasn't it?

"Race you," Juliana said.

"Where?"

"Down and back?" Juliana motioned to the end of the field with her head.

"What do I get if I win?" he asked.

Her eyes sparkled. "What do you want?"

A hell of a question. "A kiss."

She smiled. "Winner gets a kiss." The smile grew broader. "Of course, that means the loser gets one, too."

Juliana called out the count, and the horses took off, bolting at breakneck speed across the field. Webster's hat flew off his head as the cold wind rushed past him. He let out the reins, kicking Firebrand's sides, but still, Captain kept up.

The end of the field was approaching, and Webster pulled his horse in, slowing to turn Firebrand around, not wanting to risk injury to the horse by cutting the turn too tightly. Juliana and Captain surged past him, the lighter horse and rider needing less space to make the turn. By the time Webster finished turning, Juliana was nearly a quarter of the way back across the field.

He gave Firebrand his head, and the bigger horse charged forward, catching up with Captain so that the two horses crossed the imaginary finish line neck and neck.

Juliana's cheeks were flushed from the hard ride, and she reined in Captain, bringing him back to where Webster's hat lay on the ground. She slipped easily from the saddle and picked it up. The leather was smooth and worn and stained from sweat and rain.

She turned around to find Webster standing right behind her. He took his hat from her hands and slipped it onto her head.

"You're a good rider," he said.

"You're a better one," she said, pushing the hat brim back to look up at him. "You could've beat me by a length or more."

Webster shrugged. "Maybe if I knew the horse better—or the field. But maybe not."

Another man might've made sure he'd won at all costs, Juliana thought. Another man might've ignored the possible risk of injury to himself, the horse or the other rider.

"Besides—" Webster grinned, putting his arms around her waist and pulling her close to him, "—I didn't have to win to get the prize."

He bent down to kiss her and found her lips waiting for him. He tried to control his desire, afraid to come on too strong, but the feel of her body, so warm and supple against his, made him burn. He could feel her hands in his hair. This woman drove him wild. Her lips were soft, so soft, and he kissed her again and again, each time deeper and harder. He couldn't stop.

He felt her hands move around his waist. Somehow she'd taken off her gloves, and she slipped her hands up underneath his T-shirt, against the bare skin of his back. The explosion of pleasure was so intense that for one frightening moment he thought he'd totally lost control.

Then somehow, someway, they were on the ground, and he was between her legs, pressing his hardness against her. But it was through too many layers of jeans. He wanted all of her. He wanted to be inside her. But they both had on way too many clothes. Feverishly, he found the snaps of her jacket and yanked it open, running his hands over her breasts. But she wore a heavy sweater and another shirt under that. He had to touch her skin. He grabbed her shirt, pulling the tail out of her jeans. The feel of the soft, warm skin of her belly against his fingers made him groan. He jerked open the button of her jeans and wrenched down the zipper, thinking, God, he had to get these clothes off her—

But then her slim, cold fingers were on his hands. "No, Webster. Please don't," she breathed, pulling her mouth away from his. "Not like this, not here, not yet."

He swore, angry with himself as he pulled away from her. "What was I doing?" he said. "Juliana, I'm sorry." He threw himself down in the grass, on his back, next to her. And as he stared at the steel-gray sky, one arm up across his forehead, it started to snow.

He looked over at her, pulling his arm away from his face, reaching out to touch her leg, his blue eyes dark with worry. "Are you all right?"

Juliana's hands were shaking as she finished buttoning her jacket. She looked so young and vulnerable, her hair floating around her face.

"I'm sorry," he whispered again.

She reached out then and touched his face. "*I'm* sorry," she said. "I don't want to come across as some kind of tease. But I'm . . . just not ready yet. It's too much for me, Web."

He sat up, pulling her toward him, wrapping his arms around her, holding her close, feeling her heart beating next to his.

"It's okay," he murmured, watching snowflakes land on her beautiful face and hair. "We'll take it slowly. That's fine."

And the funny thing was, it *was* fine. Although he still wanted her, he was happy just to hold her in his arms. Hell, he would have been happy to sit across a table from her and simply look at her. God, he was incredibly happy.

But why? he suddenly wondered. If his feelings for Juliana were based on lust, as he'd been trying to convince himself they were, he had every right to be terrifically unhappy right now. If all he really wanted was to make love to her, then after coming so close, he should be lying here weeping, instead of grinning like the village idiot.

Juliana sighed and reached up to touch his face again, pulling his mouth down to hers.

Shut up, Webster ordered himself as he kissed her gently. *Stop thinking. Stop trying to analyze. Just be happy.*

TEN

Juliana sat at one end of the big dinner table, with Webster on her left. Alicia had prepared a delicate sautéd chicken dish, and the five friendly nuns were carefully writing down the recipe.

She looked up to find Web watching her. He was wearing his Victorian costume and looked every inch the proper gentleman—except for his eyes. The flame she could see when he looked at her was something no Victorian gentleman would have allowed a Victorian lady to see. But she was not a Victorian lady. She was a twentieth century woman. And a twentieth century woman wouldn't be alarmed by desire in a man's eyes. On the contrary.

As she looked back at him, his eyes moved from her face to rest briefly on the low-cut neckline of her gown.

"Have I told you how beautiful you look tonight?" Web said softly, his voice husky as he met her eyes again.

"Yes, and thank you, Mr. Donovan," she murmured.

In a sudden vivid memory, Juliana remembered the way he'd kissed her that afternoon. She remembered the feel of his hands on her body, his mouth against hers. Sweet heavens, if she hadn't stopped him, he would have made love to her right there in that field.

He reached out now and touched her lightly on the hand, and she looked up, startled, into his deep blue eyes. He smiled, and motioned with his head down toward Alicia, who was watching her with a patient smile.

"I'm sorry, did you say something?" Juliana asked.

"I asked if you and Mr. Donovan enjoyed your ride this afternoon," Alicia said.

Her aunt, along with the five sisters, were looking at her. They must know, Juliana thought, resisting the urge to laugh. Surely they could tell just from looking that she and Webster had spent more time off of their horses than on them. Still, she gathered herself together, and with a poise that was well-practiced, she smiled coolly.

"It was lovely, thank you," she said. "The first snowfall is always . . . special, and the cold air made the ride invigorating. It was very nice. Don't you agree, Mr. Donovan?"

Alicia watched her niece carefully, but the young woman's earlier distractedness was the only sign she'd given that something was going on between her and Webster Donovan. And the look Juliana now gave the man was nothing out of the ordinary; she was polite, almost to the point of being aloof, her eyebrow slightly raised as she waited for him to answer her question.

It was Webster Donovan's reaction to Juliana's question that made Alicia hopeful. He couldn't seem to find his voice at first, and when he did speak, he couldn't keep a certain quiet intimacy from his tone. "It was very nice, Miss Anderson," he said. "I'd love to do it again sometime soon."

Juliana stood up then to get the wine bottle from the

sideboard, but not before her aunt saw the first tinges of pink touch her pretty cheeks.

Alicia smiled. Bingo.

Late Monday morning, after the nuns departed, Alicia let Juliana finish up the dishes while she went upstairs to start cleaning the guest rooms.

As she was coming up the stairs to the landing on the second floor, Webster was coming down from the third floor.

From Juliana's apartment.

He was wearing sweat pants and a T-shirt, and his clothes were stained with perspiration. Obviously, he'd been using Juliana's newfangled workout equipment.

He smiled at Alicia easily.

"How's the writing going?" she asked.

He nodded. "Okay. I wrote all day yesterday. I actually finished the first two chapters. First draft, of course," he added hastily.

"Of course," Alicia said.

She stood there looking at him for a moment. He returned her gaze patiently, as if it was obvious to him that she had something to say, and he was willing to wait as long as it took for her to say it.

"There's something you ought to know," she finally said. "About my niece."

But he shook his head no. "If it's important, Juliana will tell me herself," he said.

The old woman smiled. "This is something that it wouldn't occur to her to say," she said, "something she might assume you already knew. And, if it's okay with you, I'd like to tell you."

She could see the indecision in his eyes, and she admired his loyalty to Juliana. He didn't want to discuss her, even with her closest relative and friend.

"Just to make this totally irresistible," she said, a glint of humor in her blue eyes, "I should probably add that what I'd like to tell you might be able to give you a pretty accurate read on her feelings for you."

He laughed. "You have no shame," he said. "And I suppose I don't either. All right, tell me."

"Juliana and I have lived in this house for five years," Alicia said. "In all that time, there's only been one other person besides me that she's invited into her apartment." Alicia looked at him pointedly.

"Me?" he said, unable to totally believe it.

"Uh-huh."

He shook his head. "What about that friend of hers—Liz?"

"Nope. You're the only one."

Alicia could see the wheels turning in the young man's head as he realized the implications of what she had told him. She left him standing there in the hallway, smiling to himself.

Juliana caught up with Alicia in the second guest bedroom and began helping her strip the bed.

"You're going to that shindig up at Beckwith's this evening, right?" Alicia said, tossing the dirty laundry in the big yellow basket. "I'm assuming you won't be home for dinner."

"Yes," Juliana said, looking across the bed at her aunt. "Alicia, do you want to come along? You know you'd be welcome."

The old woman shook her head. "Not this time," she said. "I'm taking advantage of the fact that we have no guests—besides Webster Donovan, that is— and I've signed up for a sunrise hike up Sleeping Giant Mountain. I'll probably be asleep even before you get back tonight. I've got to leave the house at four-thirty to get to the community center in time to make the bus. Ironic, isn't it? Have to take a bus in order to take a hike."

Alicia was doing this on purpose, Juliana knew. She

was making herself scarce, making it easier for Juliana's evening out with Webster to end whichever way she wanted it to. And Juliana knew exactly how she wanted the night to end. That is, if Webster was willing.

The past two nights, he'd kissed her good night, and his kisses had been sweet and tender. Yesterday evening, they'd sat on the couch in front of the fireplace for nearly two hours after everyone else had gone to bed. They'd talked softly, held each other, kissed. She'd thought maybe he would have asked her to come up to his room, but he hadn't.

Tonight, she thought, with a smile that didn't go unnoticed by Alicia.

Juliana stepped out onto the porch. The evening air was almost warm, a big change, considering that two days before it had been snowing. But the snow had only been flurries. It had only been a foreshadowing of the winter that was coming, and now they were safely back in autumn.

Webster stood up, the porch swing rocking gently behind him as he walked toward her.

He wore a clean pair of jeans and a teal cotton button-down shirt underneath his denim jacket. His hair was neatly combed, and his cheeks were so smoothly shaven she had to fight the urge to touch his face.

But why fight it, she thought with a smile. The moment her fingers touched him, his eyes softened to that shade of blue she had come to know so well. He was going to kiss her.

And kiss her he did.

"Hi," he whispered, looking down at her, his arms wrapped around her waist.

She smiled up at him. "How'd the writing go today?"

He shrugged. "Okay. I would've rather been with you."

Juliana frowned teasingly. "You're so easily distracted. How did you ever manage to write your first book?"

"It was easy," Webster said. "And I didn't know what the word *distraction* meant until I met you."

His words were light, matching her teasing tone, but his eyes were serious. Juliana stood on her toes and kissed him, her hands slipping up into his thick, dark hair.

"Hey," he said, pulling back and trying to look stern. "Stop that. It took me a long time to comb my hair. It was perfect."

Juliana laughed. "No, *now* it's perfect. Now it looks like you've been kissed. It's very . . . sexy."

Webster felt a surge of heat. "You're the one who's sexy," he said softly, his eyes sweeping her body.

She was dressed almost identically to him in blue jeans and a denim jacket. But her jeans hugged her curves and the slender lengths of her legs. She did look outrageously sexy, particularly since it had been days since he'd seen her wear anything but her long, Victorian skirts. She wore the same black tank top she'd worn that night at Red's bar, and he couldn't wait for her to take off her jacket so he could touch the smooth skin of her arms and shoulders. To top it all off, her beautiful hair was loose around her face. It gleamed in the light from the porch lamp.

She seemed embarrassed, though, and he mentally cursed himself. He was supposed to give her time and space, not constantly remind her that she drove him crazy with longing.

"Did you remember your bathing suit?" she asked.

He smiled. "I'm wearing it under my jeans," he said. "Do they really have an indoor pool?"

"They really do," Juliana said, hoisting a backpack onto one shoulder. "I packed us some towels."

Down in the driveway, Webster headed for his car, but she stopped him.

"Let's walk," she said. "It's only about a mile, and this way, we don't have to pick a designated driver."

Webster smiled. "Okay with me."

As they walked down the long, straight road that led to Sam and Liz's modern house, dry leaves crunched under their feet. The evening air was still, and smelled like autumn. Web took a deep breath. You couldn't get air like this in downtown Boston. He liked it here in the country. He really did.

He glanced at Juliana. Even in the darkness, her hair shone and her eyes sparkled as she smiled at him. God almighty, forget the air. The reason that he liked it here so damn much had nothing to do with the wide open spaces of the farms or the fresh air. It had to do with Juliana.

He was in love with her.

He could still feel his body go into partial shock whenever he thought about it. But there was no denying what he felt. It was love.

At first he thought maybe it was a crush, but he'd had crushes on beautiful women before. And those crushes had never lasted more than a week, and certainly not as long as he'd been living at the bed and breakfast. His relationships with those women had also been shallow. He'd been content to know almost nothing about them, content merely to look at them, make love to them.

And as much as he was dying to make love to Juliana, he was also dying to get inside her head, find out what she thought, what she felt.

Last night they'd sat in front of the fire for hours. He didn't pressure her. He didn't try to sweet talk her into coming upstairs with him. Hell, he didn't even try to get to second base. And he didn't do those things because he was happy simply to sit and talk to her.

And as cynical as he was, as jaded as he was, he was forced to admit that what he felt for this woman was love. He even looked the word *love* up in his dictionary to double check.

"You're so quiet tonight," Juliana said, her soft, clear voice cutting into his thoughts. "Are you thinking about your book?"

"No," he said. The sound of their footsteps on the road matched the sudden drumming of his heart. He wanted to tell her. He wanted her to know, but he wasn't sure he could actually say the words.

Webster touched her arm. "Juliana . . ."

They both stopped walking. He pulled her to him, and she came willingly into his arms.

There was a sliver of moon that appeared now and then from behind the thick clouds that were rolling in from the west. The silvery light lit Juliana's face as she looked up at him, making her look ethereal, like a wood sprite or a fairy. Her smile was enchanting, and unable to speak, he kissed her.

I love you. That's all he had to say. Three little words. Simple, right?

Wrong. He couldn't do it.

"Juliana," he murmured into her soft curls. "I wish you could read my mind."

She looked up at him, eyes bright in the darkness. "Sometimes I think I almost can," she said.

They walked the rest of the way to the Beckwiths' holding hands.

ELEVEN

Liz grinned at Juliana. "So where is he?"

Juliana smiled. "He's out in the garage, where the band's setting up. After we ate dinner, I made the mistake of introducing him to Marty and Hal, and between the three of them, they have a mutual-admiration society going. I excused myself when the conversation started turning into a debate about literature versus lyrics. I had to leave before they began a line-by-line critique of 'Achy Breaky Heart.' "

The tiny blond woman laughed. "Well, don't you dare skip out before I meet him. You're going to marry this guy, Jule. I feel it in my bones."

Juliana crossed her arms. "You know, Liz, not everybody needs to get married to live happily ever after. Take me, for example. I don't want to get married. I have no intention of getting married, not now, not ever. How many times have I told you this?"

Liz thought for a moment. "Two million?"

"At least."

"So what about Webster Donovan?"

"Webster Donovan is due to leave in a little less than three and a half weeks," Juliana said. "He'll probably come back from time to time, and I've got to confess I'll look forward to his visits. But it's not going to be permanent, Liz. So don't set yourself up for a disappointment, okay?''

''You've already disappointed me, but I'll get over it,'' Liz said.

Juliana looked at her friend closely. Liz looked tired, and she shifted in her seat as if she were uncomfortable. ''How are you feeling?'' Juliana asked. ''Lousy, huh?''

''Now the doctor's saying three more weeks,'' Liz said, rolling her eyes. ''I may not make it. I hate to complain, but every time I try to sleep, this baby stomps on my sciatic nerve.''

''Let's go into the pool,'' Juliana said. ''You can float for a while.''

''You don't mind?''

Juliana smiled. ''Just give me a minute, and I'll put on my bathing suit.''

Webster wandered around the Beckwiths' big house, searching for Juliana. There were so many famous faces around he felt as if he were in the heart of Nashville instead of a small New England town.

But it was Sam Beckwith's thirty-fifth birthday, and since Liz was too pregnant to travel south for a party, Nashville had traveled to Sam and Liz. They had many, many good friends; that much was very clear.

Webster ran into Sam in the kitchen. The country singer was restocking a cooler with beer from the refrigerator. He wiped his right hand on his jeans before holding it out. ''I don't believe we've met.''

''I'm Webster Donovan,'' Web said, giving Sam's hand a firm shake.

''I know who you are,'' Sam drawled, a twinkle in his eyes. ''You're Jule's friend. Liz told me you were tall. She's so tiny, she thinks anyone over five eleven's a giant, but for once, she's actually right. Wanna beer?''

"Thanks," Webster took the bottle Sam held out. "You don't happen to know where Juliana is, do you?"

Sam laughed. "Have you noticed that all the single men've disappeared?" he said. "That's 'cause that lady of yours is in the swimming pool. If I were you, son, I'd get my ass down there double-time."

Juliana. In a bathing suit . . .

"Which way?" Webster said.

"West wing," Sam said, pointing. "Just follow this hall down past the greenhouse and through a set of double doors. Follow your nose after that."

"Thanks—and happy birthday."

Sam looked up to thank him, but Webster was already gone.

The pool was beautiful. The room was all muted southwestern colors—pinks and beiges and soft oranges. The pool itself was sparkling turquoise blue. Plants were everywhere. Webster was reminded of Juliana's apartment.

He scanned the crowd quickly, looking for her, pulling off his shirt and boots, and stepping out of his pants. He tossed his clothes on a nearby chair.

There was a bar set up in the corner, along with tubs of beer on ice. Webster put his empty bottle in a barrel marked Recyclables, and grabbed another beer.

There was a CD player in another corner, and a man in a bright-orange bathing suit stood sifting through a pile of CDs. He looked vaguely familiar, and as he put on a song and turned away from the table, Webster got a clear look at his face, but still didn't recognize him.

It wasn't until the man started dancing the jitterbug that Web realized who he was. He was the handsome sheriff, the one who'd danced with Juliana at Red's—the one who was dancing with her right now.

But Webster forgot all about being jealous as he looked at Juliana. She was wearing a bikini. It was brightly patterned with pink and blue and yellow streaks of color. The top was little more than two triangles of fabric tied on with string around her neck and around her back. Her skin was smooth and fair, and Webster felt his chest tightening. God, he wanted to touch her.

She had a beach towel tied around her waist, and as the Sheriff spun her around and around, it flared open, revealing the long, slender legs he'd dreamed about so often.

How on earth, he thought, was he going to be able to have an intelligent conversation with this woman? How was he going to be able to stand next to her without pulling her into his arms and running his hands up and down her body?

Webster wondered if anyone around him realized the sweat on his upper lip wasn't from the heat and humidity of the room. He swiped at it with the back of his hand and took another swig of his beer. She was going to come over here and expect him to be able to actually put words together into sentences. He was going to have to stand here and not touch her.

The song ended far too quickly. He was totally unprepared. And Juliana came toward him, a beautiful smile on her beautiful face, her eyes lit with pleasure, her chest still heaving from exertion. He could see the hard buds of her nipples pressing out against the fabric of her bathing suit.

"Can I have a sip of your beer?" she asked, and silently he handed her the bottle.

Web watched her drink, watched her lick her lips as she handed the bottle back to him. Her hair was still slightly damp from the pool. He wanted to touch her so badly, he was going to have to—

Juliana put her arms around his neck.

He was still holding the bottle of beer in his right

hand, but his left hand snaked out around her waist so fast it was as if it had a mind of its own. His fingers traveled up and down her back, exploring her smooth, silky skin. He could feel her stomach pressing against his, her barely clad breasts against his chest. And suddenly touching her wasn't enough. He wanted to kiss her. He *had* to kiss her.

"You want to dance or swim?" she asked him, smiling up into his face.

Make love, he thought. He wanted to make love.

The music playing was soft and slow. "Dance," he managed to say.

Juliana stepped back, taking the bottle from him and putting it on a nearby table. He had that look in his eyes, she realized, that soft look that meant he wanted to kiss her. So she took his hand and led him onto the crowded area of the room, reserved for dancing. Then she was in his arms again, and she pulled his head down and kissed his soft lips. She could feel his surprise—surprise which turned quickly to pleasure. She could also feel his restraint. He was carefully holding back.

Good thing, she thought, stifling a laugh, remembering the way he'd kissed her out in the pasture, when he *hadn't* held back.

"You *can* read my mind," Webster said softly, smiling down at her as they moved slowly to the music. "You knew I wanted to kiss you."

Juliana felt the heat of his skin, the hard, smoothness of his muscular shoulders under her fingers. She let her hands slip down to his bare chest, and heard him take a deep, steadying breath. She smiled to herself. It was time for him to start realizing he should leave his restraint behind when they went home tonight.

"Can you read *my* mind?" she asked, looking into his deep-blue eyes. She pulled her hands back up around his neck, pulling her body a little bit closer to his. She moved her hips slightly, letting herself brush against him. Sweet heavens, he was already aroused.

His hands pulled her hard toward him, and she felt him like a rock against her. His eyes burned with a fire that was almost savage.

"God, I hope so," he breathed, before his mouth came down on hers.

His tongue swept into her mouth with a passion that left her breathless.

She was aware that they were standing in the middle of a makeshift dance floor, but she didn't stop him. He was all that she wanted. For right now, she had to remind herself. This was perfect. *They* were perfect together—for right now.

"Juliana, let me come to your room tonight," Webster said when he could finally speak, still holding her tight, no longer even pretending to dance.

But she shook her head. "No."

Oh damn, he thought. He'd done it again—pushed too far, too fast. Now what? Should he apologize, or just let it go?

"I'll come to your room," she said, looking up at him, her greenish eyes filled with desire. Pulling his head down again, she kissed him. The passion he tasted in that kiss was searing, igniting him with a need he couldn't believe would ever be fulfilled.

"Do you want to go?" Juliana murmured, resting her head against his chest, listening to the wild pounding of his heart.

"Yes."

"But you didn't get a chance to swim yet," she said, looking up at him, trying to hide a smile.

He laughed, a low, dangerous sound. "I don't want to swim," he said. He kissed her again, as if to prove his point.

By the time they'd thrown their clothes back on over their bathing suits and dug their jackets out of the pile on one of the guest rooms' beds, it had started to rain. And as Juliana and Webster stepped out onto the porch, the gentle rain became a deluge.

Juliana started to laugh.

"I guess we should wait 'til it lets up," Webster said. "What do you think?"

She slipped her arms around his waist, twisting one of her jean-clad legs around his. "I think that you're not wearing your leather jacket," she said, smiling. "And I think that rain can't hurt denim. What do *you* think?"

A slow smile spread across Web's face. "I think I've never wanted to get home faster in my entire life—rain or no rain."

Juliana held out her hand, Webster took it, and together they plunged off the porch into the pouring rain.

They were both soaked almost instantly. By the time they reached the wide front porch of the bed and breakfast, there was a river of icy water streaming down Juliana's back. Her boots, and Web's, too, were covered with wet sticky leaves.

She pushed Webster back onto the bench by the front door and pulled his boots off. Sitting on the wooden floor of the porch, she gave him first one of her own booted feet, then the other, letting him return the favor.

"Let's leave our wet clothes out here," she said, unfastening the buttons of his jacket with her icy fingers. "I'd rather not take the time right now to mop up the mess these wet things would make on the foyer floor."

"Good idea," he said, huskily, trapping her between his long legs and kissing her. His face was cold from the icy rain, but his mouth was warm and sweet. As he kissed her, he pushed her jacket off her shoulders and fumbled for the button at the waist of her jeans.

Her own fingers unbuttoned it quickly, and she pushed the wet pants off her legs. Webster pulled his shirt over his head without bothering to unbutton it, then gasped as her cold fingers unfastened his pants. She smiled as she pulled the jeans off his legs.

And then, wearing only their bathing suits, they were inside the house.

It was dark and quiet. Juliana locked the front door behind them. Before she could turn around, Webster had swept her up in his arms and was carrying her up the dimly lit staircase.

"Oh, Webster, how Neanderthal," she laughed, but he silenced her with a kiss.

She half expected him to kick the door to his room open, but he opened it the conventional way, still holding her in his strong arms.

He stopped short just inside the door.

There was a fire blazing in his fireplace.

He looked down at her, a smile on his face. "Are you responsible for that?"

She smiled, shaking her head no.

"Alicia," they both said together.

"This must mean she approves," Juliana said. That thought made her almost deliriously happy. Alicia had never liked Dennis, and Juliana had thought her great-aunt would have it in for any man who got close to her. Obviously, she was wrong.

Webster slowly set Juliana down, crossing to a bouquet of roses that sat on his dresser. "Alicia is a romantic," he said.

Juliana grabbed two towels from the chair next to the bed. She handed one to Webster, then moved the screen from in front of the fireplace. Kneeling down in front of the flames, she tried to catch the warmth it threw off.

Webster ran the towel over his body, then up over his wet curls, watching the firelight reflecting off her skin. Feeling his eyes on her, she looked up at him and smiled.

"For someone who was in such a hurry to get home, you're standing awfully far away," she said.

Her tone was light, teasing, but he could see that she was just as nervous as he was. And still he didn't move any closer.

She ran her own towel through her hair, looking into his blue eyes.

He turned suddenly, taking the thick bedspread off his bed. Juliana helped him spread it in front of the fireplace, and then he knelt next to her.

"I'm afraid that once I start touching you," he said, his voice low, "I won't be able to stop. I'm afraid I'll lose control."

He drew in his breath sharply as she leaned forward and kissed him. Her lips were soft, delicate against his. They brushed against him lightly as she spoke. "At the risk of sounding wanton, I've got to confess . . . I bought a box of condoms. It's upstairs. We have ten—"

"Twenty," Webster said.

Juliana pulled back to look at him, one eyebrow raised teasingly. "Rather sure of yourself, weren't you?"

He laughed. "Only hopeful. Desperately hopeful."

She looked into the fire pensively. "Twenty condoms," she mused. "Do you think we can use them all before Thursday—before my next guests are due to arrive?"

"Definitely." His voice was husky.

"Then," she said, a smile in her eyes, "as long as we're planning to make love twenty times, I think it would be rather nice if you could manage to lose control at least once or twice."

Webster looked at her. Her hair was starting to dry, and it created a halo around her face. Her skin was so smooth, and the light from the fire created shadows that emphasized the full swell of her breasts.

"Touch me," she said, the fire reflecting in her eyes, "and don't stop."

Slowly, so slowly, he reached out and slid his fingers down the warm skin of her arm and then back up to her shoulder and under her hair to her neck, then to her face. He touched her lips gently with his thumb, then leaned forward and kissed her. His hand moved down to her throat, to her collarbone, his fingers trailing lightly between her breasts. His mouth followed close behind. Gently he cupped one full breast, and with a moan, she leaned into him.

It was all the invitation Webster needed. Two swift yanks were all it took to untie her bikini top, and he tossed it quickly away. Her breasts were beautiful, round, and full, and he buried his face in them, latching onto one hard nipple with his mouth, encircling it with his tongue, sucking until she cried out with pleasure.

She pulled his mouth up to hers, and as she kissed him fiercely, he pulled her onto him so that she was straddling his lap. His hands massaged her breasts, her back, her derriere, even as her own hands explored his athletic body. He pressed her against him, pushing up with his hardness, leaving no doubt in her mind how badly he wanted her.

Juliana moved her hips against him, and suddenly she was on her back. She felt him, hard between her legs, pushing, straining against their bathing suits. The rush of emotions nearly overwhelmed her. They were actually going to do this. They were finally going to make love. Sweet heavens, this was so much better than anything she'd imagined. His handsome face looked down at her, filled with desire and hunger for her—for *her*.

He took her nipple into his mouth again, and sweet pleasure shot through her. She arched her back, pressing up toward him.

Breathing hard, Webster pulled at her bathing suit bottom, and she lifted her hips to help him remove them. She looked up at him, momentarily meeting his eyes. They were hot and wild and deep, deep blue. He swept his gaze down the length of her slender body, as if he could caress her with just a look.

She pulled him down toward her, crying out as electricity rocketed through her from his touch. She kissed him again and again, locking her fingers in his thick, dark hair.

Webster couldn't stop. She moved underneath him, wanting him, ready for him. Somehow he got his bathing suit off. And then her hands were there, touching him, stroking his length, helping him sheath himself with the condom. He heard himself moan and he pushed her down onto the blanket, underneath him.

Her hands were on his back then, pulling him to her, urging him on. With a ragged cry, he plunged into her, swallowed by her soft, warm wetness.

Juliana lifted her hips, welcoming him, loving the way he filled her.

"Oh God," he moaned and, looking down into her eyes, began to move with a rhythm that she matched.

He kissed her, driving deeper and harder into her. Nothing—nothing had ever felt like this. In the firelight, she could see the muscles standing out in his powerful arms and chest. She touched him, feeling the steel beneath his smooth skin.

"Juliana," he gasped. "I can't stop."

But she didn't want him to stop. She wrapped her legs around his back, opening herself wider to him, and kissed him, pulling his tongue hard into her mouth. She was so close. . . .

"God," he breathed. "Oh Juliana, I'm going to . . ."

She wasn't sure exactly what happened, whether it was a coincidence of timing or the sudden rush of the turn on she got from his softly spoken words, but she exploded just as he did. It spun her, carried her, swirled around her—a wild, scorching, ferocious release. She heard herself cry out with pleasure, the sound of her voice intertwining with his.

Then Webster lay heavily on top of her, and she quietly stroked his hair as their breathing slowed. Juliana smiled softly to herself. That had always been a major part of her fantasies about him—that they would make love, and she would climax with her fingers buried in his gorgeous hair.

He rolled over, pulling out of her and wrapping her in his arms.

"Can you read my mind now?" he murmured, brushing her hair back from her face.

Juliana looked up into his soft blue eyes. The softness was such a contradiction to the hard planes and angles of his face. Still, she could see contentment in those eyes—contentment and satisfaction and . . . love. He loved her. She had no doubt of that. A shiver went down her spine.

"Yes," she whispered. "I can." She smiled. "Any second now, you're going to kiss me."

"Absolutely uncanny," he murmured, doing just that.

TWELVE

When Juliana woke up, the sun was already high in the sky. Webster's big arm was across her as they lay like spoons in his bed. He was breathing quietly and steadily, and she slipped away from him, getting out of the bed to go into the bathroom.

She looked at herself in the bathroom mirror. Her hair was a wild mass of curls, and her eyes looked a little sleepy. But the smile on her face was satisfied. *Very* satisfied. She borrowed some of Webster's toothpaste and brushed her teeth with her finger.

She'd finally found the perfect man. He was smart, funny, handsome, kind, sweet, caring, and he made love to her with a passion that she'd never imagined possible. And on top of all that, he lived a life that allowed him time to travel. Juliana smiled again, thinking Webster could come out to Benton to write several times a year. Write, among other things.

Yes, this had real potential for working out, Juliana thought. She'd have her own life, he'd have his, and occasionally the two would intersect.

She went back into the bedroom to find that Webster was awake. He smiled at her from the bed, watching her naked body moving toward him, with a desire in his blue eyes that he didn't try to conceal. When she got close enough, he grabbed her, pulling her back down under the warm covers with him.

He kissed her—a long, sensuous kiss that left no doubt in her mind what he had planned for the rest of the morning.

She pulled away from him, trying to frown, but not quite succeeding. "*I* have today off," she said. "But aren't you supposed to be writing or something?"

"Or something," he agreed, pulling her on top of him and kissing her again.

"At this rate, you're never going to finish your book," Juliana laughed. "You told me your goal was to finish the first twelve chapters before you leave."

"My new, immediate goal is to keep you in this bed with me until Thursday," Webster said, his hands sweeping her body.

"Thursday? Don't you think we're going to get a little hungry?"

"We can send out for pizza." He grinned.

She smiled back. "I think you're just procrastinating."

He shook his head. "Procrastinating is getting the urge to do something unpleasant instead of writing, like cleaning out the refrigerator or putting captions in all your old photo albums. Making love to you is *not* procrastination."

Now Juliana shook her head. "The definition of the word has *nothing* to do with the unpleasantness of the task that you do while you're procrastinating. It's simpler than that. You *should* be writing, and you're not. Therefore, you're procrastinating."

Webster swung his long legs out of bed, vanishing into the sitting room. He came back seconds later, carrying his dictionary. Sweet heavens, he was a beautiful man, Juliana thought, forgetting all about their conversation. His legs were long and lean, leading up to narrow hips. He was solid, not all elbows and knees like many tall men. She shivered, remembering how it felt with his weight on top of her. His body was like that of a professional athlete, with muscles that bulged enticingly in all the right places.

He sat down on the edge of the bed, flipping through the big book.

"What do you do to stay in such good shape?" she asked.

He glanced up at her, still leafing through the dictionary. "In Boston, I belong to a fitness club. Two nights a week, I play with a basketball league. The rest of the time, I get into pickup games. Oh, here, look." He pointed to the page of the dictionary. " 'Procrastinate,' " he read. " 'To put off intentionally, habitually, and reprehensibly—' Ooh, that makes it sound so nasty, doesn't it? '—the doing of something that should be done.' You were right. No mention of cleaning the refrigerator. Unless that's what they meant by reprehensibly."

Webster closed the dictionary, putting it down on the floor next to the bed. "I guess I'm guilty," he said. "Although, for the record, I *have* finished eight chapters."

Juliana stared at him. "*Eight* chapters! When? You've been with me almost every day."

He crawled under the covers, kissing her. "What d'ya say we get some wood and make another fire?"

She laughed, squirming away from him. "Don't change the subject!"

"What d'ya say we skip the wood," he said, pinning her down and grinning devilishly. "The implication being, of course, that we make each other."

"*Make* each other?" Juliana said, eyebrow lifting delicately. "How romantic."

Webster kissed her again slowly, and Juliana felt herself melt against him. "Oh, yeah," he said, his voice thick with desire. "I'm very romantic. I'm a writer, remember? Romance is one of my specialties."

"You're a writer," Juliana agreed, trying hard to keep the conversation on track despite his wandering hands. "Which brings us back to your eight chapters. You've been writing all night again, haven't you?"

Webster tried another kiss, but it only distracted her momentarily.

"Haven't you?"

He shrugged. "Not all night. Just—"

"Most of the night," she finished for him. "Webster, you've *got* to sleep sometime."

He smiled charmingly. "Hey, I slept last night."

Her eyebrow was up again. "You mean that you were in *bed* last night. If I remember correctly, neither one of us did too much sleeping."

"Sometimes I think I don't really need sleep."

"*Everyone* needs sleep," Juliana said. She frowned up at him suddenly. "I hope that you don't think I'm nagging, or being bossy."

He smiled at her, his eyes suddenly soft. "No," he said, "I like it that you care. I like it a lot."

Juliana propped her head up on her hand, her elbow resting on the pillow as she looked at him. "I *do* care," she said, then smiled. "But my motivation is kind of selfish. I'm afraid if you don't sleep, you'll get sick again. And to tell you the truth, I'd rather spend my time making love to you, rather than holding your head while you hurl."

Web shouted with laughter. *"Hurl!"* he said. "That's one word I'll bet you don't use when you're throwing your fancy dinner parties."

"On the contrary," Juliana said, very proper. "In fact, it's an old, Victorian term—"

Webster grabbed her, tickling, and she exploded in laughter. But her laughter soon turned to a sigh as his caresses grew more intimate.

"Juliana, I've never been so happy," he said, kissing her soft lips.

"Webster Donovan," she whispered, "let's procrastinate. . . ."

Juliana went down to the kitchen at four o'clock in the afternoon to get them some food. She was making sandwiches, standing at the counter in Webster's bathrobe when Alicia came in from outside.

"There's some cut-up fruit in the fridge," the older woman said.

Juliana blushed. "Thanks."

"There's a load of jeans and jackets in the dryer," Alicia added. "And I cleaned off the boots and put 'em in the mud room."

"Sweet heavens, I forgot all about that stuff," Juliana said. "Oh, Alicia, thanks. You didn't have to—"

"I know, I didn't," Alicia said, going into her own room. "Must've been one hell of a night," Juliana heard her say before she closed the door.

"Let's go out," Webster said, his blue eyes reflecting the firelight. Outside the window, the sun was beginning to set.

Juliana sat up and looked at him. "Out?" she said, her eyebrow rising. "As in actually put on clothes and go outside of the house?"

He grinned at her lazily. "Clothes, yeah," he said. "We gotta get back into the habit of wearing them, especially considering that tomorrow morning you've got to go back to work. Besides, after we get home tonight, I can take 'em off of you."

She laughed. "Aren't you tired of me yet?"

The words were said teasingly, but Webster answered her as if she had spoken seriously. "Jule, I'll never be tired of you. I'm going to want you until the day I die," he said quietly. "And probably even after."

She smiled at him, but her smile was shaky, and her voice caught in her throat when she spoke. "That's a nice thing to say."

He shook his head. "I didn't say it to be nice," he said. "I said it because it's God's truth. It's a fact. You better never leave me, lady, 'cause I'll turn into one of those sad, old cowboys in a country song, sitting in a bar, crying into my beer and carrying a torch for the rest of my lonesome life."

"Webster, I'm not going anywhere," Juliana murmured, kissing him.

"This time, let's *really* go out," Webster said, glancing at the clock. "Come on, it's almost nine, let's go down to Red's, grab a beer and something to eat. Maybe some of Sam's Nashville friends are still around. Marty told me that when they come to town, they like to go into Red's and jam. You and I can dance."

For about five minutes, he added to himself, looking down at the gorgeous woman in his arms. After only five minutes of dancing, he'd want to take her back here and undress her really slowly.

"Take me for a ride on your Harley," he said.

Juliana looked up at him. "You're kidding."

"No, I'm not."

"You're awfully large," she said skeptically.

"Why, thank you," he said, waggling his eyebrows.

Juliana made a face at him. "Riding a bike has to do with balance," she said, pulling out of his arms and sitting up. "I'm used to riding with a hundred and twenty-five pounds on the seat. You're talking about adding another . . . what? Two hundred?"

"Almost. One ninety-seven," he said.

"Have you ever been on a bike before?" she asked.

"Once or twice," he said.

"How's your balance?"

Webster fell over onto his side. "Perfect," he said.

She smiled down at him. "It's cold out there. You better wear leather."

Juliana pushed her Harley onto the driveway, under the big spotlight, as Webster came out the back door. She went back into the garage, and returned carrying two helmets. She was wearing her black leather riding jacket and a pair of black pants. She handed him a helmet.

"Oh my God," Web said. "Leather pants. Forget the bar. Let's go back inside."

She laughed. "I thought you'd like 'em."

"*Like* 'em?" he said. "It's beyond like." He fell to his knees in front of her and ran his hands down her legs. He lifted her knee, bringing one tightly clad thigh toward his mouth. "I have to bite you."

"Later." She smiled, gently kicking free. "I don't want teeth marks on the leather."

She slipped on her helmet and made sure his was properly fastened, then got on the bike. Webster climbed on behind her. "While we're riding," she said, "don't distract me."

"Who me?" he said.

"I'm serious, Webster," she said. "I'm going to need you to lean with me. Keep your hands around my waist. Believe me, anywhere else is distracting."

Guiltily, he moved his hands from the butter-soft leather that covered her thighs.

"Where are your gloves?" she asked.

"I lost 'em."

"Put your hands under my jacket," Juliana said.

The temptation was too great. His hands strayed upward.

Juliana turned around and looked at him. He couldn't see her eyebrows under her helmet, but he knew one was raised.

"Sorry." He grinned, obviously not sorry at all.

She adjusted some of the controls, then jumped on the kick start. The big motorcycle roared to life.

Webster could see the flash of her white teeth through the protective windshield of her helmet as she looked back at him one more time.

She revved the engine, and they were off.

So far, so good, thought Juliana as they came to the end of the driveway. The light from her headlight bounced against the dead leaves of the bushes across the way. There were no cars out, so she pulled slowly onto the road, taking her time, getting used to the feel of the bike with so much additional weight on the back.

Last time she'd carried a passenger, it had been Liz, back before the woman was pregnant. And tiny Liz barely weighed ninety-five pounds, maybe one hundred on her bad days. With a roar, Juliana gunned the bike past Liz and Sam's house.

The night was cold, but the road was dry. Juliana smiled to herself, remembering the last time she'd been on this road, running home with Webster in the torrential rain. Had it really been two days since they'd even been out of the house?

She slowed as she approached the familiar sign for Red's, and pulled carefully into the pothole-ridden parking lot. She stopped the bike next to the building, then pulled off her helmet, turning around to look at Webster.

"What do you think?"

"It was great," he said. "Let's go home."

He moved his hands from around her waist. One hand went up, the other went down.

"Webster," Juliana laughed, pushing his hands away.

"I can't help it," he said, taking off his helmet. "You make me incredibly horny."

"How can a man who's just spent the past forty-eight hours doing nothing but making love and sleeping *possibly* want more sex?'' she asked, shaking her head.

"At this point, it doesn't have anything to do with hormones,'' he said. "At this point, it's psychological. See, I'm . . . um . . .''

"This is going to be a good one,'' Juliana smiled. "Come on, you can tell me. No, wait, I think I know. You're mentally linked to aliens who are using you in a study on human sexuality, and they're continuously stimulating your brain in such a way as to make you feel constantly aroused.''

Webster thought about that. "Nope. It's more complicated than that.''

"Okay,'' she said. "I give up. You're what?''

"I'm . . .'' he started, then stopped.

Webster gritted his teeth and closed his eyes tightly for a moment, and when he opened them, she was struck by how very blue they were.

"I'm in love with you, Jule,'' he whispered.

Juliana's heart almost stopped. She'd never expected him to admit it. Not so soon. Maybe not ever.

He was looking at her with so much trepidation on his face she almost felt like laughing. Almost.

Instead, she kissed him.

And then she took him home.

THIRTEEN

Thursday morning, Juliana climbed out of Webster's bed at six-thirty, trying not to wake him. But a strong hand snaked out, grabbing her and pulling her back into the warmth of the bed. She found herself looking into a pair of sleepy blue eyes.

"It's not *really* Thursday, is it?"

She smiled. "It really is. There are two million things to do today before the guests arrive. I know Alicia would appreciate my help."

"Is there a dinner tonight?" he asked, lazily entwining his legs with hers.

"Yes," she said, trying to pull away. "Webster, I really have to get up."

He kissed her, then let her go. "When do they leave?"

"The guests?" Juliana smiled, finding her panties on the floor and pulling them on. "The people staying in the blue room and the ones in the gold room leave Monday morning. The couple in the green room are honeymooners. They're here 'til Friday."

"And that's when the next guests arrive," Webster said, trying hard not to pout.

Juliana pulled her shirt on without bothering to put on her bra, then stepped into her leather pants. She stuck the bra into her jacket pocket, then leaned over Web to kiss him good-bye.

He caught her face between his hands. "Jule, I want you in my bed at night," he said. "Do you think, maybe . . . ?"

"It's one thing for me to sleep down here when there are no other guests in the house," she said, her face serious. "But Webster, think of my reputation." She shook her head. "Sweet heavens, imagine if one of these guests is the newspaper reviewer. Can you picture the kind of review I'd get if they saw me sneaking in and out of your room at all hours of the night and morning?"

"But you've got couples coming, not a reviewer," he said. "Really, Juliana, I know. The reviewer isn't—"

"It doesn't matter," she interrupted. "Come on, Web, it's my reputation we're talking about here. Many of my repeat guests enjoy coming here because they appreciate the fact that we observe the proprieties. They like the whole Victorian feel of this house—and I'm talking about more than the architecture."

"Let me move my computer up to your room," Webster said. "I can stay up there. I won't come down, and no one will even know I'm there."

Juliana looked at him sharply. He was actually serious. And she couldn't squelch the panic that rose in her at the thought of him living with her up in her apartment. "No, Web."

He must have realized how desperate his words had sounded, because he waggled his eyebrows, and said, "I can be your love slave."

"It wouldn't work."

"Yes, it would," he said, but still, she shook her head. "Why not?"

Juliana looked away from him, unwilling to tell him that she didn't want him up in her apartment with her. For him to use her workout gear was one thing. For him to live up there and make love to her was entirely different. She grabbed at the easiest excuse. "Because . . . I've got formal dinner parties tonight, Saturday night and Sunday afternoon. And if you're locked in my apartment, you won't be able to put on your Victorian clothes and help me with the guests."

Webster nodded, disappointed but accepting. "All right."

"Next Sunday," she said, smiling.

"What?"

"Starting next Sunday," Juliana said, "you'll be the only guest here until the following Friday. It's the last week of your stay. If you use this week while the other guests are here to finish your book, then starting next Sunday, I'll come in here and lock this door, and we won't even come up for air."

A slow smile spread across Webster's face. "Is that a promise?"

"Absolutely."

Juliana went into her office, her long skirt sweeping behind her. She hadn't set foot in here in days, she thought guiltily, pulling her correspondence file and leafing through it quickly. She had to remember to sit down with Alicia and go through this stuff. A logo and letterhead she recognized as belonging to the *Boston Globe* caught her eye, and she moved that letter to the top of the pile before laying the entire file down on her desk.

A folded piece of paper directly in the center of her desk caught her eye. Frowning slightly, she carried it into the kitchen.

"Alicia," she said, and her great-aunt looked up

from the row of pies she was baking. She held up the piece of paper. "This was on my desk."

Alicia was nearly elbow deep in pie crust. "Put my glasses on my nose for me, will you?" she asked.

Alicia's reading glasses were hanging by a chain around her neck. Juliana slipped them onto the older woman's face.

"It's addressed to you," Alicia said.

Juliana slowly opened it up, holding it out for Alicia to look at.

"It's signed, 'Webster,' " Alicia said. "Looks like some kind of love letter. You want me to read it to you?"

Juliana shook her head, refolding the letter.

"I guess this means you haven't told him," Alicia said dryly.

Juliana looked unhappily at her aunt. "He thinks I'm perfect, Al," she said. "And you know, when I'm with him, I can pretend that I am."

Alicia stopped rolling out the dough and focused all of her energy into the look she gave her niece. "You *are* perfect," she said. "Just a little different."

It was the stock reply that Alicia had first given her all those years ago, when Juliana had been a rebellious, angry teenager, feeling woefully inadequate and inferior. She couldn't read She was sixteen years old, and she couldn't even read "See Spot run," like a first grader. She was stupid. She'd heard it so many times from the other kids, even from the teachers, that she had started to believe it herself.

"Remember," Alicia said. "You're not stupid. You're dyslexic. There's a difference."

Juliana smiled. Down through the years, that had been Alicia's other war cry.

Her smile was the correct response, and Alicia turned some of her attention back to the dough.

Juliana folded the note from Webster and slipped it into her skirt pocket, then washed her hands.

"I'm wondering why you haven't told him," Alicia said.

Juliana didn't answer for a long time, helping Alicia lift the delicate pie crust into the pie tin.

"I think it's because I'm afraid Webster won't accept that I can't read," she said quietly. "His whole life is built around words, Al. I'm afraid he'd push for me to go back, see what advances they've made in teaching dyslexics to read." Her voice got even softer. "I don't want to do that again. I've failed enough. And I've managed to get by just fine *without* being able to read."

Alicia smiled at her great-niece. She could remember the first time she'd met the scrawny kid with wild red hair and anger on her face. Her lawyer had gotten hold of the girl's file for her—her school records, the police reports. It had been so obvious to Alicia what the problem was, yet Juliana had never even heard the word *dyslexic* before. But even after that, despite creative teaching and learning techniques, the girl still hadn't been able to learn to read.

Alicia knew it hadn't been from lack of determination or will, because the child had plenty of those. She wanted to read so badly she made herself physically sick. That was when the specialists all came to the same sad conclusion. Juliana's dyslexia was so severe, they'd said, she'd probably never learn to read. She'd make better use of her time, they told her, by learning how to get around the written word.

And that's exactly what Juliana and Alicia did. With the use of audio tapes and telephone answering machines, they set up a system of communication and learning that worked quite well. Alicia read her favorite books into a tape recorder until her voice was hoarse. Then she got her friends and *their* friends to do the same. She took Juliana on trips, brought her face to face with historical places and natural wonders that other children only read about in books.

Juliana's dyslexia only affected the way her brain processed letters. She could read numbers most of the time, provided they were clearly displayed. And the girl was an absolute whiz at math.

But many times over the past twelve years, Alicia would read about some new method researchers were using to teach dyslexics, and off Juliana would go, the sacrificial guinea pig. The last time had been over five years ago, at that foolish boy Dennis's request. Because her fiancé had wanted her to, Juliana had gone twice a week to a Harvard laboratory where she and fourteen seven-year-olds worked with some of the country's leading special education teachers.

When Juliana broke off her engagement to Dennis, she dropped out of the program and told Alicia that she was through wasting her time trying to learn to read.

"I guess you'll just have to make it clear to Webster how you feel," Alicia said calmly.

"But if he really wants me to try again," Juliana said slowly, "and I don't, then he'll think . . ."

"That you don't love him?" Alicia finished for her. Juliana blushed.

"He probably knows that you love him by now," Alicia said, "unless, of course, that's another thing you haven't bothered to tell him . . . ?"

"Um," Juliana said.

Alicia laughed, shaking her head. "Good Lord, I can remember being young and foolish, too. Well, I guess you've got to do it your own way. Lord knows *I* did."

Juliana swept into the front parlor, the perfect Victorian hostess. Her hair was piled on top of her head, off her smooth, creamy shoulders. She was wearing the blue evening gown with the low neckline that revealed the tops of her full breasts. Breasts that Webster had caressed, kissed, tasted. . . .

Web crossed his legs, suddenly glad that he was sitting down.

She moved further into the room, and he watched her greet each couple, holding out her hand, smiling, calling them by name. She was perfect, exactly what he'd expect a beautiful but very proper Victorian lady to be. Slightly aloof, with a hint of holier-than-thou thrown in for good measure. He smiled at a sudden, very vivid memory of her naked body gleaming in the firelight, her eyes sparkling as she smiled up at him as she touched him most intimately.

God almighty, it had only been two nights since she'd shared his bed, since they'd made love, and he was damn near tied in knots with frustration. Only two nights, and he was ready to scream. And if he couldn't handle only two nights, there was no way on God's earth he was going to pack up his things and go back to Boston when his six weeks were up.

He'd thought about it endlessly during the past two sleepless nights—when he wasn't thinking about Juliana's long legs or the look of pleasure in her eyes when he touched her a certain way.

He'd finally told her he loved her. He'd finally made the words come out of his mouth. And he wrote her that note so she'd understand the things he couldn't bring himself to say. And as he put it all down on paper, he realized he was doing more than explaining how he felt to Juliana. He was also clarifying his feelings in his own mind.

He didn't believe in love, yet he'd gone and proven himself wrong. He'd been skeptical at first, but he loved her. He really, truly loved this woman. And he wanted to be with her.

He wanted to marry her.

Except he didn't believe in marriage. Happily ever

after was only the way fairy tales ended. It simply didn't apply to real life.

He'd seen enough of his friends' marriages break up after five or six years—some in even shorter time. And he'd seen enough of his parents' friends, married for twenty-five, thirty years, apathetically plodding through life, attached to their spouses with an air of resigned indifference.

No, he didn't believe in marriage.

But he still wanted to marry Juliana.

He wanted to try.

He wanted to prove himself wrong again.

She was walking toward him, now, her hand outstretched, smiling politely, her eyes distant.

Webster got to his feet to take her hand, raising her fingers lightly to his lips. As his mouth brushed her warm skin, he saw her eyes spark, and he smiled.

"Good evening, Mr. Donovan," she said.

He inclined his head slightly. "Miss Anderson," he murmured, and as she looked one more time into his eyes, he knew that *she* knew he wanted desperately to tear her clothes off and make mad, passionate love to her.

"Shall we go into the dining room?" Juliana said. "Mr. Donovan, if you would act as my escort this evening . . . ?"

She slipped her hands into the crook of his arm, and he covered it with his big fingers. They hung back as the guests began filing out.

"You know this is killing me," he murmured. He pulled her closer to his side, so that their legs were pressed together, so that her breast brushed against his arm. "Absolutely killing me."

Juliana smiled at him in her most Victorian fashion, but as soon as the last of the guests had left the room, she turned and kissed him fiercely. His hands pulled her against him, and she could feel his erection, even through all their layers of clothing.

"I have an idea," he said, kissing her mouth, her cheeks, her eyes. "Tonight, after everyone's asleep, we can sneak out of the house and drive over to Stockbridge and get a room at a motel."

Juliana laughed. "Webster, that's brilliant, but I can't just leave. What if something happens? What if someone needs me?"

"*I* need you," he said, his voice husky.

"I'm sorry," she said. "I really am." She kissed him again, gently this time. "Take me in to dinner please, Mr. Donovan."

Webster sat on Juliana's right at the dinner table. He was a hit, as always, with his charming manner and his flair for starting conversations that were more than mere small talk. But every time he looked at her, his eyes gave her a clear message.

He wanted her. And even if they stood up and went upstairs right this second, it wouldn't be soon enough for him.

"How's the writing coming, Mr. Donovan?" Alicia asked from the other end of the table.

"Very well, actually," he said. He turned to look at Juliana, his eyes lingering on her face. "As a matter of fact, I'm estimating I'll finish my first draft before next weekend."

"Oh, that's *great*," Juliana enthused, just barely catching herself before she called him Webster. "I mean, that's *wonderful*, Mr. Donovan."

As she looked up at him and saw the pride and pleasure lighting his handsome face she wished desperately that there was some way they could find some time to be alone.

Juliana lay awake in her bed, thinking about Webster Donovan.

She could still feel his lingering kiss good night. She could still feel his arms around her, pulling her close. She could still hear his voice, whispering her name. She could still feel the fire he could ignite deep inside her with just one word, just one look.

Turning over, she looked at the clock. The digital numbers read 1:57. Damn. She had to get up in less than four hours. Double damn.

How weak could her body be, she wondered. She'd spent, what? Three days, three nights with Webster? How could her body have gotten so used to him so quickly that now that she wasn't with him, she couldn't sleep?

Sex sure was a funny thing, she thought, adjusting her pillow, trying to get comfortable. Five years of celibacy, and she'd been fine. No problem. Well, hardly any problem. Then, whammo, Webster comes along and suddenly she's unable to sleep.

No fair.

Alicia looked up from washing the dishes as Webster came into the kitchen.

He looked like hell.

His hair was standing straight up, as if he'd spent the entire night running his hands through it in frustration. His eyes were rimmed with red, and he hadn't shaved. He wore his old, torn sweat pants and a faded T-shirt that had definitely seen better days.

"You missed breakfast," Alicia said.

"No kidding," he muttered, taking a mug from the cabinet and pouring himself a cup of steaming black coffee. He took a sip, then grabbed a dish towel from the pantry door and started drying the dishes in the rack. "I actually managed to fall asleep at quarter after five this morning. Mind if I forage?"

"Help yourself," she said, taking the towel out of

his hands. "I'll do that. You're a guest, remember? For now, anyway," she added.

He squinted at her suspiciously. "If that's a snide remark, I'm way too tired to understand it."

Alicia laughed. "Sit down, I'll make you breakfast."

He brought his coffee over to the kitchen table, lowering himself into one of the chairs as he grumbled, "Are you sure? I wouldn't want to break any house rules."

"Shoot," Alicia said, hands on her hips. "*You're* in a bear of a mood this morning."

Webster folded his arms on the table, then rested his head on them. "I'm sorry," he said, his voice muffled. "I'm exhausted."

"You should've stayed in bed."

He turned his head to look at her. "Yeah, well, I woke up," he said. "I started thinking about Juliana, and it was all over. No more sleep. I figure eventually I'll just fall into a coma. Hopefully it'll be *after* I finish the book."

"Eggs?" Alicia asked.

He shook his no. "You know what I'd love," he said.

"No, what?"

Webster lowered his voice, looking around the kitchen conspiratorially. "Don't tell Juliana, but . . . I'd really love something simple, like a bowl of Cheerios or Corn Flakes."

"You got it," Alicia said, taking a cereal bowl from the cupboard and putting it on the table in front of him. She took a pitcher of milk from the refrigerator and pulled a whole collection of boxed cereal from the pantry. "Help yourself."

Webster poured Cheerios into his bowl, then added the milk and began to eat as Alicia finished drying the dishes. She poured herself a cup of coffee then and sat across from him at the table.

"So when are you going to ask her?" she said.

Webster stared blankly at her. "What?"

Alicia smiled patiently. "When are you planning to ask Juliana to marry you?"

His expression didn't change.

"You *are* planning to ask her, aren't you?"

He blinked. "Well, yeah, but how did you—"

"You don't believe I'd allow such carryings-on in my house if I didn't think you two were going to get married now, do you?"

He laughed. "Well, no, I guess—"

"I have the perfect ring," she said. "Unless you've already picked one out?"

He shook his head. "No, actually I was planning to go to the jewelers in Stockbridge tomorrow, but I don't even know her ring size or—"

Alicia knocked on the table, interrupting him. "Wait here. Don't go anywhere."

She swept out of the room, but came back only a few moments later. She put a faded velvet ring box on the table in front of Webster. "Go on," she urged him. "Open it up."

Slowly he picked it up and sprang the release. It was an emerald in a simple setting, with a small, twinkling diamond on either side of it. The band was gold. "It's beautiful," Webster said, looking up at Alicia.

She nodded. "Juliana's always loved this ring. She doesn't know it, but it was mine. It was my engagement ring."

"What happened?" Webster asked softly.

Alicia laughed, and only years of wisdom and acceptance kept her laugh from sounding bitter. "World War Two happened," she said. "You see, I met Jack in London, in 1936. He wanted to marry me the day after we met, but heck, I was only twenty-two years old. I was crazy about him, but marriage?" She sighed. "I returned to the States, and we corresponded for years. In 1939, he convinced me to come back to London. I was there when Hitler invaded Poland, and the entire world hit the proverbial fan. Jack gave me this ring, asked me to marry him, then joined the Royal Air Force. We had two days together before he shipped out for training. He died in a bombing raid over Dresden, at the end of the war.''

Webster didn't say a word. Somehow "I'm sorry" seemed so inadequate.

"Jack loved me the way you love my niece," Alicia said. "It's only fitting you give her this ring."

He nodded his head slightly, meeting her eyes. "Thank you, Alicia," he said, adding, "Next Sunday. I'm going to ask her as soon as the guests are gone."

_____ FOURTEEN _____

Sunday afternoon, Webster realized he was the only one in the house. The guests were all out, not due back until dinner time, Juliana had told him. And Alicia was visiting a friend. Juliana was working out in the garden, planting bulbs in the cold ground and raking leaves.

Ready for a break, he pulled on his jacket, about to join her outside, when he heard her footsteps coming up the stairs. He went out on the landing, only to see the door to her apartment close behind her.

He went up the stairs and knocked lightly on the door. There was no answer. He _knew_ she was in there, so he knocked harder.

Deep within the walls of the house, the pipes groaned and banged slightly as water went through them. Juliana had turned on her shower. No wonder she didn't hear him knocking.

In one great, aching flash of desire, he could suddenly picture her standing under the stream of water, rubbing soap over her naked body.

Webster pressed his forehead against the smooth wood of the door, wanting her so badly he nearly shook. He tried the knob, but it was locked, as he expected.

But he had the key.

Slowly he drew it out of his pocket and put it in the lock. It turned with a click and the door began to open. Then stopped.

There was a chain lock on the door.

Mystified, Webster stared at it. A *chain* lock.

Slowly, he closed and locked the door.

Why on earth would Juliana put on her chain lock in the middle of the day? Particularly when she knew he was the only other person in the house?

Unless it was there to keep *him* out.

Disturbed more than he let himself believe, he went back to his room.

Monday night. It was Monday night. Tuesday, Wednesday, Thursday . . . Juliana counted them off on her fingers. Sweet heavens, six more days until the last guest left the house.

She sat up in her bed, turning on the light. She couldn't stand it any longer. She wanted to be with Webster.

Most of the guests were gone. The only people left were the honeymooners, and they tended to keep mostly to themselves. They wouldn't notice if she crept down the stairs to Webster's room. They probably wouldn't notice if a tornado took the roof off the house!

She thought of Webster. His smile was so sweet. His arms were even sweeter.

She threw on a pair of jeans and a T-shirt and grabbed her key. Silently, she went out the door and down the stairs to the second floor. There was a night-light on in the hallway, and the only sound was the ticking of an antique wall clock. She crept up to Webster's door and listened.

Very faintly, she could hear the sound of his computer keyboard. It would start and stop, start and stop, go for long amounts of time interspersed with equally long amounts of silence. He was writing. He was in the sitting room, the room he called his office, which meant he probably wouldn't even hear her soft knock at all.

Juliana reached out and tried the knob. It turned. The door wasn't locked. She opened it quietly and slipped inside, careful to lock it behind her.

The spread had been pulled back from Webster's bed, as if he'd made an attempt to go to sleep, but failed. There was a pile of wood by the fireplace, but the hearth was cold. Juliana's bare feet didn't make a sound on the hardwood floor as she walked to the sitting room door.

Webster's back was to her as he sat working at the computer. He wore only a pair of briefs, and the sight of all of his muscles and smooth skin made her feel a touch faint. He stared at the computer screen, arms across his chest. He sat unmoving for several long minutes, then suddenly, he cleared the screen and sprang up out of his chair. When he saw Juliana standing in the doorway, he froze.

"You want to take a break?" she said.

He just stared at her. "Are you real?" he finally said. "Or have I started hallucinating?"

"I'm real." She smiled.

He took one step toward her. And then another. His face was troubled. "Jule, I know it might seem like I've been pressuring you to make love to me, but I understand. I really do. See, I know how important your reputation is to you, and I don't want to be responsible for putting it in jeopardy."

She shook her head. "I'm here because I want to be. Because . . . I couldn't stand it another second."

His arms were around her then, pulling her in to him, wrapping her up tightly. He brushed her lips with his, softly first, then harder, touching her teeth with his tongue, and suddenly something snapped.

Juliana wasn't sure if it was her or him or both of them, but someone's hands had unfastened the tops of her jeans, yanking the zipper open, pushing them down around her knees. As she kicked her pants the rest of the way off, he pulled her T-shirt over her head. She wore no bra, and he groaned his pleasure as his hands touched the softness of her breasts.

She wriggled out of his grasp, hooking her fingers in the elastic waistband of his shorts and pulling them off his long, lean body. Somehow, magically, Webster grabbed a condom from what seemed to Juliana like out of thin air, sheathing himself as she stepped out of her panties.

He picked her up then as he kissed her again, his big hands holding her derriere. Her arms locked around his neck, her legs around his waist. She could feel him, hard and smooth, pressing against her, ready to enter her—

"Wait!" Juliana said.

With her in his arms like this, they were practically nose to nose, and she stared into his brilliant blue eyes. "You're kidding," he breathed.

"Webster, I need to tell you that . . . I love you."

She pressed her hips down, and suddenly he was inside her. The double look of shock on his face was so intense Juliana had to laugh. But then his mouth came down on hers, and he was thrusting up into her even harder, even deeper, setting a rhythm that kept on building until it reached a wild, feverish pace.

"Juliana, my God," he gasped. "Now—"

As if on cue, her body responded with an orgasm that erupted through her, wracking her with pleasure. She met his eyes, their gazes locked as he came, too. She bit her lip to keep from crying out. Sweet heavens, there were *guests* sleeping just a few doors down!

Every nerve in his body tingled, but Webster just stood there, holding Juliana tightly, his eyes closed as he regained his breath. Her head was against his shoulder, and he lifted her off of him with muscles that suddenly felt like gelatin. Somehow, he managed to swing her up into his arms. His knees were weak, but he carried her into the other room. Sitting down on the bed, he held her on his lap. God, he loved her.

And she loved him.

Juliana felt Web's gentle hand pushing the hair back from her face, and she opened her eyes to find him watching her.

"Say it again," he said softly. "Please?"

She wet her lips nervously with the tip of her tongue, then looked up into his eyes. "I love you," she said.

His blue eyes seemed to brim with emotion. He nodded slowly. "That's what I thought you said."

"I have to go," she whispered.

"Stay with me. We can set the alarm for really early. You can leave before anyone else wakes up."

"I can't," she said, leaning against him, wishing desperately that she could. "I'm exhausted, Web, I need to sleep. And you know if I stay with you, we won't sleep."

"What if I promise you that we won't make love, that we *will* sleep?"

Juliana laughed softly. "You know darn well that within an hour or so, I'd be begging you to break that promise."

Reluctantly, she stood up and stretched, then padded into the sitting room to find her clothes. Webster followed her, leaning against the door frame.

"Let's go riding tomorrow," he said, watching her dress. "After breakfast."

She kissed him lightly on the lips. "It's a date."

She walked to the door, opening it a crack and peeking out.

"All clear?" Webster whispered.

She nodded. "Good night," she said, kissed him once more, and slipped out the door.

"Juliana." It was barely loud enough to hear, but she turned back. "You know I love you too," he breathed.

She smiled and went up the stairs.

Finally, finally, she'd be able to sleep, Juliana thought as she opened the door to her apartment. She peeled off her clothes and crawled into bed naked, but the sheets were icy. She climbed back out and got her flannel pajamas from the closet. Pulling them on quickly, she couldn't keep from thinking that if she were sleeping in Webster's bed, she wouldn't need pajamas. With the body heat he radiated, he kept the bed plenty warm.

Back in bed, she stared up at the skylight, watching the stars twinkling in the cold sky.

Okay, she thought. Now was when she would sleep. She had just made love with the man she adored, her body felt terrific, sated, wonderful, and exhausted, so now she could just close her eyes and sleep.

Juliana opened her eyes a few minutes later. This was bad. This was *very* bad. Her bed seemed so big, so empty. She missed Webster. She wanted him beside her, holding her. Forget about the sex. It didn't have anything to do with the sex. It had to do with loving him, with wanting him near her all the time. Day and night.

Damn, she thought, staring at the skylight. Double damn.

Sighing, she turned over, pounding her pillow. Well, she better get used to it. He was leaving in less than two weeks.

With Webster on Firebrand right behind her, Juliana steered Captain carefully around one of the larger patches of mud in the steep trail that led down the mountain. But without warning, the big horse skidded, losing his footing in the wet leaves and dirt.

As Captain tried to regain his balance, he tripped. She gave him his head, hoping he'd come out of the stumble naturally, by picking up his pace.

Juliana held on for dear life, as they went into a staggering gallop. She could hear Webster shouting and looked up.

A low branch.

Directly in front of her.

There was only enough time to do one thing.

Hit it.

She went down hard, into the mud. All the air had left her lungs, and she lay there, trying to draw in a breath. When she finally could breathe, she wished desperately that she hadn't bothered.

Pain shot through her—great, fiery streaks of pain with each inhale and each exhale. The sensation was unmistakable. She'd cracked a rib again.

Webster touched her gently on the face, and she looked over to see him kneeling next to her, unmindful of the thick mud. He was talking, saying something, but she couldn't hear him over the roaring in her ears.

Damn, she thought. Double damn. If she passed out now, he'd end up lugging her down to the county general hospital. All they'd do was wrap her up tight with an ace bandage like the one she already had in her underwear drawer, tell her to take a few days off, take things slow—and charge her several hundred dollars for the privilege.

Juliana closed her eyes briefly, shaking off the dizziness. When she looked back at Web, most of the roaring was gone.

"I'm okay," she said.

His hands were in her hair, gently feeling the back of her head. "You sure you didn't hit your head?" he asked, his face tight with concern.

Her face was very pale, and although she tried to smile at him, her mouth was tight. She was obviously hurting. "I'm okay," she said again.

Webster ran his hands lightly down her legs and arms, checking to make sure she hadn't broken anything in the fall. "Well," he said lightly, trying to still his own fear. "You know I'd do damn near anything just to be with you, but spending the morning sitting in the mud is kinda low on my list."

Juliana laughed weakly, then swore, clutching her side.

And suddenly Webster saw a clear replay of the accident in his mind—he saw Juliana hit that tree branch with enough force . . . to break her ribs.

He swore then, his hands reaching for the zipper of her jacket. "Let me see—"

"I'm okay." She pulled away from him, using the trunk of a nearby tree to haul herself to her feet. Her face had gone yet another shade paler, and beads of sweat stood out on her forehead and upper lip. Her hands were shaking as she tried to brush the mud and wet leaves off her jeans.

"I don't call having broken ribs okay," Webster said.

"Cracked," Juliana said. "They're only cracked."

She held out her hand for Captain, and he obediently came toward her, nuzzling her fingers as if to apologize for the spill she took.

"Yeah, well, I'll believe that when I see the X rays," he said.

"I don't need X rays," she said. "I've cracked my ribs before, I know what it feels like, and I don't need X rays."

She gathered Captain's reins and slowly began leading the horse down the trail. Walking hurt like hell, but the jostling she'd get from riding would be unbearable. One foot in front of the other, thought Juliana, gritting her teeth. Eventually it would stop hurting . . . like in a few weeks.

"Jule, wait!" Webster sprinted toward her, catching up quickly. Just as he suspected, the injury had sent her system out of whack. Her pupils were slightly dilated, her skin pale and clammy, and she shivered despite the sunlight. He peeled off his leather jacket. "Let me put this around your shoulders," he said.

She didn't argue, but she didn't move, so he slipped the soft, warm jacket around her like a cape, fastening the top button at her neck.

"Thanks," she whispered, her eyes suddenly filling with tears.

"Oh, Juliana, I'm so sorry," Webster said, reaching to draw her gently into his arms.

But she had already turned away, her attention focused on the steep, winding trail down the mountain.

Webster went back to Firebrand, quickly untied him and followed Juliana. It wasn't until they reached the open clearing of the pasture that he was able to walk alongside her. Her eyes were wet, and she angrily kept wiping them dry with the unmuddied back of her hand.

"You know, it's okay if you cry," Webster said softly. "Broken ribs hurt like hell."

"Cracked," Juliana said tersely. "They're only cracked, and I like to save my tears for the really important things."

Webster shook his head, laughing slightly in disbelief. "Oh, come on, Jule. Like what?"

"Death," Juliana said, her attention focused on the ground in front of her. "And the equivalent. This doesn't come close."

They were approaching the stable.

"Jule, I want to take you over to the hospital," Webster said.

"No, thank you."

"Come on."

"No."

"Juliana, let's talk about this."

"There's nothing to talk about," Juliana said, stubbornly leading Captain into the barn. "I'm not going."

Webster eased his Miata carefully over the bumps and potholes of the gravel driveway and made a right-hand turn onto the main road.

Juliana stared at him. "Where are you going?" she asked, knowing full well exactly where they were heading.

"I'm taking you to the hospital," he said.

Her eyes flashed. "Oh, what, now I don't even have anything to say about this?"

"You were the one who didn't want to discuss it," Webster said, his eyes just as hot. "I wanted to talk about it—"

"You wanted to sweet-talk me into doing something I don't want to do," Juliana said accusingly. "And since that didn't work, you've resorted to kidnapping."

"I wanted to tell you *why* I think you should go to the hospital," he said. "Jesus, Juliana, talk about not having a say—you act like what I think and feel doesn't count!"

"And *you* go and treat me like a child, doing what *you* think is best for me, since *obviously* I can't take care of myself!" Juliana glared at him. "Turn the car around, Webster."

"No." His profile was grim as he watched the road. "You ever hear of internal injuries, Jule? People have accidents like the one you just had, and they think they're okay, only they're bleeding internally. They end up *dying*."

"I'm *not* bleeding internally."

"Fine," Webster said, shortly. "But I'd like a second opinion."

"Damn it, Webster, if you don't turn this car around . . ."

"What?" he said, glancing over at her, his eyes crystal blue. "What are you going to do, Jule? There's nothing that you can threaten me with that'll make me risk your life. Nothing."

Juliana was still angry three hours later when Webster pulled his little sports car into her driveway. She didn't wait for him to help her out of the car. She pulled herself awkwardly and painfully out and went in the back door, not even bothering to see if he was following.

She was sitting on the bench in the mud room, trying to pull off her dirty boots when Webster came in. He crouched in front of her, taking her booted foot in his big hands.

"Don't you *ever* ask for help?" he said, pulling off first one boot and then the other.

She pushed her hair out of her face with a hand that was shaking. From anger or pain, Webster didn't know.

"I don't need any help," Juliana said.

"Jule . . ." he said, but she stood up, turning her back to him as she unfastened, then stepped out of, her mud-encrusted jeans. She shrugged painfully out of her dirty denim jacket, and left that, too, on the floor with the jeans.

Webster had managed to scrape most of the mud from his own pants, so he quickly pulled off his own boots, then followed her into the kitchen.

Alicia looked up from the stove, where she was adding chopped celery and potatoes to a pot of bubbling pea soup. Her eyes widened as she saw Juliana. "What happened to *you*?"

"I cracked a couple of ribs," she said.

"*Broke,*" Webster said. "You *broke* them."

"He dragged me to the hospital," Juliana told Alicia

indignantly, "even though I told him I was okay. And now he's refusing to apologize."

"I'm sorry that I upset you," Webster said softly. "But I'm not going to apologize for doing the right thing."

"Oh, and *your* way is automatically the right way," Juliana said. She started to cross her arms, but thought better of it as a knifelike stab of pain shot through her. "You know, Webster, sometimes you can be a totally obnoxious jerk."

Webster turned away, but not before Alicia saw the hurt in his eyes. "Yeah, well . . ." he said. He smiled tightly. "Gotta live up to my reputation."

He left the room, the door to the hallway swinging shut behind him. Alicia was silent as they listened to his footsteps go all the way up the stairs, and down the hall. The door to his room opened and closed before she looked at Juliana.

Juliana swallowed.

Alicia was looking at her the same way she had back when Juliana was a teenager and had broken one of her great-aunt's rules. The older woman's face was stern, her eyes stormy.

"You know darn well that if you had come home without going to that hospital, miss, I'd've made you turn around and go right back," Alicia said. "You had no right to make that young man feel so terrible."

"You wouldn't have made me go to the hospital, because I wouldn't have told you I was hurt," Juliana said tiredly, sitting down carefully at the kitchen table.

"Oh, that gives me great comfort," Alicia said, shaking her head. "*Great* comfort." She crossed her arms and glared down at Juliana until the young woman met her eyes. "I've known you for twelve years, Juliana. You've always been fiercely independent, sometimes too much so for your own good. Sure, going to the hospital was a pain in the neck. But that's too bad.

You needed to go, and you should have accepted it. And if you couldn't have accepted it for your own health needs, you should've gone out of deference to Webster.

"Independence is more than simply doing everything alone. Because there are certain times when even the most independent person needs an extra hand—or an extra opinion. You've got to learn to give a little up, trade a little in, because sometimes there's strength in numbers."

Juliana stared down at the table, pain etched into her delicate features. Alicia laid a gentle hand on her niece's shoulder.

"Go take a shower," she said. "And call me if you need any help putting on that ace bandage. They *did* give you another ace bandage, didn't they?"

"I told them I still had the one I used last time," Juliana said. She stood up, smiling wryly. "I couldn't see being charged God knows how many dollars for something I already had."

"Well, call me if you want some help," Alicia said, turning back to her soup. "Of course, I'm sure Webster would be more than willing to give you a hand, provided you started the conversation with an apology. . . ."

FIFTEEN

Webster sat in front of his computer, staring out the window. He'd showered and put on a clean pair of jeans and a T-shirt, and now he just sat there, not writing.

It was long after lunchtime, but he wasn't hungry. He felt like maybe he'd never be hungry again. Not as long as Juliana was angry with him.

He had to apologize. But how could he sincerely tell her he was sorry when he'd turn right around and do the very same thing again if she hurt herself tomorrow?

And there was more to it than that. There was more that was bothering him. Webster was starting to get a nagging suspicion that Juliana maybe didn't see their relationship in the same light that he did. The way she'd reacted to him today—it was as if she felt her health and well-being were none of his business, as if he had no right to intervene.

And that scared him.

It scared him the same way that chain lock on her apartment door had scared him.

He wanted to play an active part in every aspect of

her life, yet there were times and places where she would shut him out.

Webster closed his eyes, and for the first time since he was a little boy, he found himself praying. *Please God,* he thought, *just let her know how much I love her.*

There was a soft knock on his door.

Alicia or Juliana?

Please God, let it be Jule.

Webster cleared the computer screen and went to the door. Slowly he opened it.

Juliana.

She wore a soft, white bathrobe and her hair was clean and still a little damp. Her feet were bare, and her face looked pale and exhausted.

God, she looked so good. He realized he was staring at her.

"If you're working," she said softly, "I can come back later—"

"No," he said quickly. "Are you kidding? Please, come in. I've been sitting here, hoping that you'd come down." He glanced at her, and she could see a flash of misery on his face as he added, "I didn't want to come upstairs and risk getting you madder at me."

"I'm not mad at you," Juliana said. "I mean, I *was* angry, but I shouldn't have been— Web, if I don't sit down, I'm going to fall over."

Quickly, his arms were there, around her, carefully holding her up as he half led, half carried her over to the bed.

"You should be in bed," he said, sitting next to her. He closed his eyes as he felt her relax against him, his arms still around her.

Thank you, God, he thought. *Thank you, thank you, thank you.*

"I had to talk to you," she said. "I wanted to . . . um . . . Webster, I'm really sorry about—"

"Shhh," he said, kissing the top of her head. "It's all right."

"No, it's not," she said, pulling back to look into his eyes. "I was wrong, and I was rude. And I *am* sorry."

Webster smiled, his eyes soft. "I love you," he said, thinking, gee, it was getting easier and easier for him to say this. "Even when you're wrong and rude, I love you. Which, I have to add, only seems to happen when you've got a set of broken ribs. If you broke *my* ribs, you'd see a lot more than rude, *that's* for sure."

"I guess that means you forgive me," she said.

He kissed her. "Absolutely."

But she still looked uncertain, unsure of herself. "I wanted to ask you . . ." She moistened her lips and started again, looking up at him. "I, um, need your help."

If he was surprised, he hid it well. "Anything, Jule," he said, his voice husky.

"Last time I cracked a rib," she said, "I got into bed and then I didn't move for two solid days. Will you do me a favor and help Alicia with the breakfasts?"

"No problem."

"And the other thing . . ." Juliana said, taking a large ace bandage from the deep pocket of her robe. She held it out and met Web's soft blue eyes. "I can't do this myself."

Silently, he took the elastic bandage from her, and unfastened her robe, helping her pull it off her shoulders. She was wearing a soft flannel nightgown underneath with a long row of tiny buttons down the front. His large fingers unbuttoned them deftly, exposing her full, round breasts and the ugly bruise on the lower side of her ribcage.

"Jesus, Jule," he breathed. There was an angry, red mark where she'd actually come into contact with the tree branch. Around it, her skin was dark purple, with spots of yellow and even green.

He began wrapping her, starting directly underneath her breasts and slowly winding the bandage down until it covered the painful-looking bruise. He fastened the ace bandage carefully with two little metal clasps.

Juliana's eyes were closed and she was breathing really shallowly, as if it hurt to take a deep breath. "Oh, Web," she said, her voice cracking slightly, "it really hurts."

His arms went around her, so gentle and strong. "Did you take some of the painkiller the doctor gave you?"

"Yeah," she murmured. "Right before I came downstairs."

"It should start working soon, baby," he said. "Any minute now." His hand was stroking her hair soothingly. Juliana closed here eyes.

"Web, please," Juliana said softly, "can I stay here? Will you hold me for a while?"

She felt him move her so that she was lying down. His arms were still around her, his body nestled against hers. He covered them both with the bedspread.

And then Juliana felt the painkiller she'd taken kick in. Her ribs still hurt, but now the pain was dull, manageable. Her head felt heavy, and she knew it was only a matter of moments before she'd be asleep. As if from a distance, she thought she heard Webster murmur, "Jule, if you'll let me, I'll hold you for the rest of our lives."

Juliana sat on the porch swing in the sunshine, a blanket wrapped around her shoulders, watching the Beckwiths' Wagoneer pull up the driveway. Sam got out and helped Liz down from the front seat, then helped her walk up to the porch.

"Hey, Jule," he drawled. "How're the ribs?"

Juliana smiled. "Better. Just don't make me laugh too hard."

"Who would've figured," Liz said, making herself comfortable in the wicker rocking chair, "that between the two of us, with me being nearly nine months pregnant, I'd still manage to be less of an invalid. I think you did this on purpose so you wouldn't always have to be the one to visit me."

"Yeah, right," Sam said, winking at Juliana. "Liz never got a busted rib. She doesn't realize it's not the sort of thing you'd want to do on purpose. I'll swing by in about an hour on my way back from town, all right, ladies?"

Liz lifted her face for a good-bye kiss, and then Sam was gone.

"So," Juliana said.

"So," Liz said. "How's you-know-who?"

"Did I hear someone mention my name?" Webster said, bringing two mugs of tea out onto the porch.

"Well, if it isn't the world-famous author," Liz said, taking one of the mugs. "Thank you. Aren't you supposed to be writing?"

As Liz watched, Webster handed the second mug to Juliana. Her sharp eyes didn't miss the way he tenderly touched her hair before he sat down on the bench across from them.

"I finished," Webster said, still looking at Juliana.

Liz snuck a glance at her friend. Jule was smiling back at the man as if they had some kind of a secret. Hmmm.

"It's only a first draft," Web added. "But there's a lot there that I'm proud of."

"He read it to you yet?" Liz asked Juliana.

She shook her head in exaggerated disappointment. "No. And he says he's not going to." She sighed. "I guess I don't rate first drafts."

"Oh, come on," Webster said. "No one reads my first drafts."

Alicia stepped out onto the porch, dressed in her long, black overcoat, and matching hat. "I'm off then," she announced. "Hello, dear," she added as she saw Liz. "How are you? Getting close, isn't it?"

"Not close enough," Liz said darkly. "The doctor's *still* giving me another week. I've entered the final phase of pregnancy—the loss of hope phase. I'm convinced it's just never going to end. I'm going to be pregnant forever."

"I had a friend once," Alicia said. "She was four weeks overdue. That was forty years ago, back before they started inducing labor."

"Cheer me up, why don't you," Liz groaned, shaking her head. "It's time to change this unpleasant subject. Where are you going, Al?"

As soon as she asked, she figured it out. Alicia was clearing out to give these two—the two who only had eyes for each other—a chance at some privacy.

"A friend of mine just went into the hospital, down in Manhattan," Alicia said. "I'm going to visit her and some other friends in the city."

"Don't tell me," Liz said. "This is the friend who was so long overdue. After forty years, she's finally going to have the baby!"

Juliana gave a strangled laugh. "Oh, ouch! *Don't* make me laugh, Liz!"

"Sorry!"

"I'll see you at the end of the week," Alicia said, kissing Juliana. She winked at Webster, ruffled Liz's golden curls and went down the stairs.

Liz waited until Alicia was out of earshot, then leaned forward. "Jule, you know I adore Alicia, but every time she leaves, I always feel like, 'All right! Mom and Dad are away, let's have a *party*!' You know what I mean?"

Juliana smiled. "That's because you never went through a truly rebellious phase."

"Only because my parents were great," Liz countered. "How could I be rebellious when whatever I did was perfectly okay with my parents—short of death and dismemberment of course."

"Liz really does have tremendous parents," Juliana told Webster.

"And five perfect brothers and sisters," Liz said. She grinned. "And then there was me and Batman."

"Batman?" Webster frowned.

"Kurt," Juliana explained.

"You know, the dark knight," Liz said. "Even as a child, that boy was not normal. He was always brooding."

"*Kurt?*" Webster said. "Happy, friendly Kurt? *Brooding?*"

"Yeah. But mom and dad still loved him," Liz said.

Inside the house, the telephone rang.

"You want me to get it?" Webster asked.

Juliana nodded. "If it's for me, can you bring me the cordless phone?"

"I am your slave."

Liz could tell his words weren't entirely in jest. She watched him smile at Juliana and touch her face gently before he went inside.

"This guy is crazy about you," she whispered to her friend. "It's *so* sweet."

Juliana blushed.

Webster appeared in the doorway. "Jule, it's the Edgewoods," he said. "They've got a family emergency in Ohio, and since Horace won't fly, they were hoping to stay here." He paused. "Tonight."

Juliana stared up at Webster. His face was expressionless, but she knew he wanted her to say, no, they couldn't come. He'd asked her out to dinner tonight to a fancy restaurant in Stockbridge. If the Edgewoods were coming, they wouldn't be able to go. Add on top of that, with Alicia out of town, they'd been looking forward to having the entire house to themselves.

"What kind of emergency?" she asked.

"Mrs. Edgewood's mother died," he said.

Juliana swore softly. "How can I turn them down?" she said. "I'm sorry, Web. Can we go out tomorrow night?"

He nodded, smiling. "I'll tell 'em we'll be waiting for them. But you're not cooking dinner. You're still not up to that."

He turned away, but then turned back, coming out onto the porch. " 'Scuse me, Liz." He put his two large hands over the blond woman's ears. "I may go into severe withdrawal if you can't manage to sneak down to my room tonight," he said to Juliana, then let go of Liz.

"I keep my promises," Juliana said, and Webster nodded, a slow smile spreading across his face.

"What promises?" Liz asked as soon as Webster was gone.

"I promised Web . . . some time alone, just the two of us, when he finished his book," Juliana said tactfully.

Liz grinned. "I remember when Sam broke a rib in that celebrity rodeo," she said. "We had to make love *real* slowly and carefully. It was great."

"Liz!" Juliana laughed, then grabbed her side.

"It *was*!"

"What was?" Webster asked, coming back onto the porch.

"Nothing!" Both Liz and Juliana said it at the same time, and Juliana's cheeks turned pink.

"Now that's an admission of guilt if *I* ever heard one." Webster stretched his long legs out in front of him lazily as he sat on the bench. "Who are you guys talking about?"

"Actually, we were talking about Sam," Liz said, with a grin at Juliana. "He's got a charity concert somewhere near Springfield tomorrow night. It's at Holyoke, I think. Or one of those colleges up there."

"Do you have someone coming to stay with you?" Juliana asked.

Liz shrugged. "Mom and Dad are right in town if I need 'em. Besides, Sam'll be back that night. Late, but he'll be back." She smiled. "To tell you the truth, I'm hoping that his being out of town will tempt fate, and I'll actually go into labor. At this point, I just want to have this baby."

Juliana glanced up to find Webster's eyes on her. One more week, she thought suddenly. He was leaving in one more week. Maybe he'd stay longer, finish up another draft of his book.

No, that was ridiculous, she realized. He couldn't just stick around forever. But before he left, she was going to set a date for her to visit him in Boston. And maybe this winter, he could come up and go skiing.

She smiled. If she had that to look forward to, his leaving would be okay. Yeah, it was going to be okay. . . .

SIXTEEN

Juliana sat at the kitchen table, waiting for her coffee cake to bake.

"Okay," Webster said, breezing into the room. "The Edgewoods are all set. I did everything but tuck 'em in."

"They looked exhausted," Juliana said. "Poor Mrs. Edgewood. I feel badly for her."

"Can I help you with anything?" he asked, gently massaging her shoulders.

She smiled up at him. "You can sit down and help me wait for this cake to finish baking. The Edgewoods want to leave the house by five, and they told me not to bother getting up. So I thought I'd bake a coffee cake tonight and leave it out for them. I'll also set the timer on the coffee maker." Her smile turned slightly wicked. "That means you and I can stay in bed, guilt free."

"Guilt free." Webster nodded, sitting across from her and taking her hand. "I like that."

Juliana's hair was shining, and the dark circles of pain that had remained under her eyes for days had finally vanished. Webster smiled, remembering how she'd stayed in his room—in his bed—for the past week, just letting herself rest and heal, letting him take care of her.

Every night, he'd slept with her in his arms. They hadn't made love, but it didn't matter. It was enough to hold her, to be next to her.

"Have you heard anything about a storm coming?" Juliana asked, standing up and opening the oven door, checking on the cake. Another five minutes, she thought.

Webster shook his head. "No. Why?"

"Mr. Edgewood told me there's supposed to be a storm coming in tomorrow, heading down from Canada. That's why they want to get on the road so early. It's supposed to hit Ohio pretty hard. He said they were predicting fourteen inches of snow."

"If we get anything, it'll probably just be rain," Webster said. "It's too early for any major snow, isn't it?" He laughed. "God almighty, wouldn't that be a pain in the neck? Our big chance for some time alone, and we get snowed in with the Edgewoods."

Careful of her ribs, Juliana sat down on his lap. She put her hands up around his neck and played with the hair that curled over his collar, kissing him softly on the lips. "Are you going to make love to me tonight?" she asked, looking into his deep-blue eyes.

He kissed her, and she could taste a hint of fire. "That depends," he said. "How do you feel?"

"I feel . . . all right," Juliana said. She looked at him out of the corner of her eyes. "I'd *like* to feel better."

Webster laughed—that soft, dangerous, sexy sound that she loved. He kissed her again, and his kiss held promises of things to come.

Juliana looked into his eyes again. There were times like this that she loved him so much she seemed to lose all sense of balance. If she weren't holding on to him, she'd probably fall right over.

"Thank you for not making a fuss about missing our dinner date," she said softly. "It means a lot to me to be able to help the Edgewoods. I love you," she added, her voice even softer.

He gave her another kiss, one so sweet and soft and slow that time seemed to stand still around them. But time *wasn't* standing still, and that coffee cake was going to burn unless it came out of the oven.

Gently slipping out of Web's arms, Juliana stood up, crossing to the oven. She peeked inside, then turned off the heat and grabbed the oven mitts. She carefully set the pan down on the cooling rack, then closed the oven door.

"That's it," she said. "Just let me check to make sure I set the timer for the coffee maker . . ."

"Juliana, will you marry me?"

She turned around, staring at him. She must have misunderstood. "I'm sorry, what did you say?"

Webster stood up, and Juliana felt her head tilt back as she looked up at him. Sweet heavens, sometimes she forgot exactly how tall this man was.

"I wanted to ask you after we got back from dinner," he said, his eyes intent. But then a smile softened his face. "I kind of pictured us sitting in the front parlor in front of the fireplace, wearing fancy clothes. I wanted it to be perfect, but I also wanted to ask you tonight. So here we are, wearing our jeans, in the kitchen, with the Edgewoods upstairs. It may not be the most romantic setting, but God, Jule, I love you, and I can't wait another minute to ask you. I want to marry you. Say you'll marry me."

Marry me.

Juliana laughed, very faintly.

Marry me.

His words seemed to echo, bouncing off the walls of the kitchen.

Marry me.

He was standing there, waiting for her to say something.

Marry me.

"Um," Juliana heard herself say.

Webster laughed. "Not exactly the response I was hoping for, but it's a start."

"Webster," she said, and her voice sounded weak to her own ears. She cleared her throat and leaned back against the kitchen counter for support. "I'm sorry, but . . . no."

It was not the answer he wanted, and his smile disappeared. "What?" Now he was the one hoping he'd misunderstood.

"No," Juliana repeated softly. "Thank you, but . . . no."

Webster stared at her, confused and shaken. The tone of her voice had been so very definite, so absolute. She didn't want to marry him. "Why not?" Somehow he managed to keep his voice sounding calm.

Juliana was looking down at her feet. When she looked up at him, he saw she was as unhappy about this as he was. "Webster, I thought you knew," she said slowly. "I don't want to get married. I like my life the way it is. I like being independent—I don't have to answer to anyone. Marriage would change all that."

She really didn't want to marry him. Really, truly, absolutely, she didn't want to marry him, and she had a bevy of excuses lined up and ready to explain why.

"There's just no room in my life for marriage," she said.

Something snapped. Getting mad wasn't going to help, Webster tried to tell himself. But he couldn't keep the words from coming out. "You mean, there's no room in your life for *me*," he said. "Jesus, Juliana, you *just* said that you loved me—"

"I *do* love you," she protested.

"Yeah, just not enough," Webster said, unable to keep the bitterness from his voice.

"That's not fair," she said, her voice shaking. "Did you really think I'd be willing to just give up this place, my life? Did you really think I'd just throw it all away? Damn it, Webster, I'm *happy* living here."

"So instead, you're going to throw away what we have between us," he said angrily.

"We can still see each other," Juliana objected. "I can come to Boston to visit, you can come out here and write a few weeks each year—"

"A few *weeks*," Webster's voice was getting louder. "I don't want a few lousy weeks. I want every second, every minute. I want day and night, Juliana. I want it enough to be the one to make all the concessions. *I'll* move out here, I'll come to you, we can do it your way."

"Webster, I don't want to get married," Juliana said. "Not to you, not to *anyone*. I just don't want to!"

He was silent then. She could see the muscles working in his jaw.

"Well, I do," he finally said. "And I don't want to do this halfway. I'm not interested in a long-distance, part-time relationship. I want it all—or I want nothing."

He turned and walked out of the kitchen.

Juliana lay in her own bed for the first night in close to a week. She didn't sleep. Her eyes were wide open, staring out through the skylight into the night sky.

She wished desperately that she had been able to make Webster understand. She'd planned out her life, and it all worked out very nicely for her without a husband. She was content here, with things exactly as they stood. And how many people could say that they were really, honestly content?

So why did she feel so damn unhappy?

And why did she miss Webster so much?

He's only downstairs, she told herself, trying to dismiss it. She'd see him tomorrow.

Except he was going to leave, and she'd never see him again. All or nothing, he'd said.

All or nothing.

Both prospects scared her to death.

If Alicia were here, she would recommend something she called "the rocking chair test." "Pretend that you're one hundred years old," Alicia would say, "and you're sitting out on your front porch in a rocking chair. Now think back on your life. What was it like? Do you have any regrets?"

Juliana thought about spending the next seventy years without Webster, and she almost couldn't breathe. It would be awful. She would learn to live without him; that much she knew. But memories of his face, his smile, the soft light in his eyes—those memories would haunt her throughout the years.

And, yes, when she was one hundred years old, she certainly would regret having let him go.

Now she closed her eyes, imagining herself sitting in that chair, and suddenly Webster was there, sitting beside her. His hair was a thick shock of white, and his face was lined, but his eyes were still the color of the sky, and his smile could still make her heart beat faster.

She imagined a life married to him. She could picture him spending his days writing as she tended to the guests. She saw him sitting across from her at the dining table, dressed in his Victorian suit, a dark lock of curls falling dashingly over his forehead. She could hear his voice and the voices of her guests calling her "Mrs. Donovan." She could picture him up here in her apartment—*their* apartment—every night. Watching movies, working out, making love. . . .

Winter, spring, summer and autumn, he'd be there all year long. She could picture them out in the yard, building a snowman with the . . . children? She could imagine them with children, Juliana realized with a start.

She smiled, picturing sweet-faced babies and toddlers with curly black hair and deep-blue eyes.

She could imagine her love for Webster growing stronger as the years went on. She could imagine standing by his side, his arm around her, her arm around him.

She could imagine a happiness unlike any she'd ever known. And it would be happiness, not merely contentment.

All or nothing, he'd said.

Heaven help her, Juliana thought. She was going to marry him.

SEVENTEEN

The morning sky was overcast with heavy gray clouds. Juliana paused outside of Webster's door, but there was no sound from within. Slowly, she turned the knob, pushed the door open, and peeked inside.

The shades were drawn, and the room was dim. Webster lay fast asleep in the middle of his bed, one arm thrown up over his forehead. The blankets were a rumpled mess around him, as if he'd been tossing and turning.

Juliana quietly backed out into the hall and closed the door. She'd let him sleep. She was feeling well enough to run out and pick up a load of firewood downtown, and she wanted to check in on Liz.

She smiled. If Webster was still asleep when she got back, she'd wake him up.

Webster stared at himself in the bathroom mirror. God almighty, he was hungover. *This is what you get,* he silently berated himself, *for staying in a house where all they have to drink is brandy.* A hangover from drinking too much brandy was much nastier than a good, clean beer hangover. Well, maybe not, he thought, but it sure seemed that way right now.

Slowly he rinsed his face and brushed his teeth, and then went downstairs in search of coffee. He found a pot on the warmer and poured himself a cup.

There was no sign of Juliana, but he didn't expect to see her. No doubt she was hiding up in her room. Hiding from *him*.

He was so depressed. How could she not want to marry him? If she really loved him, how could she bear for him to leave? His stomach churned at the thought of not seeing her every morning, of not being able to hold her in his arms at night. How could she not feel it, too?

Unless she didn't love him.

Sure, she said she did, but no two people have exactly the same interpretation of a word. When he said, "I love you," he meant that he couldn't live without her, that he burned for her, body and soul. Maybe when she said the same words, she merely meant that she enjoyed being with him, that for this moment in time, he gave her pleasure.

Or maybe it had all been a lie.

He took the jewelry box with the engagement ring out of his pocket and stared at the faded velvet cover. He might as well put it back in Alicia's room.

But her door was locked.

He went back into the kitchen and slowly sat down at the table. Opening the box, he looked at the beautiful ring. She wasn't going to marry him. And he didn't want anything less from her.

This is what he deserved for being stupid enough to fall in love in the first place, Webster thought. Love didn't work. It just didn't work.

He had to get out of here. He had to pack up his things and leave. He couldn't stay, not another minute.

Webster snapped the jewelry box shut. He'd leave this in the office, inside Alicia's desk drawer.

The tiny office was dark, and there was no overhead light, so he switched on the small lamp that sat on the first of the two desks. Juliana's desk.

There was a folder open, and as he glanced down, the letterhead from the *Boston Globe* caught his eye. He picked up the letter, reading it quickly.

Then, frowning, he read it again, more slowly this time.

It was standard correspondence, and it announced the impending arrival of one Webster Donovan, representative from the *Boston Globe*. The letter went on to inform the Misses Dupree and Anderson that Mr. Donovan would be reviewing their establishment for an upcoming article and accompanying book on New England's bed and breakfasts.

All this time, Juliana had known he was the reviewer, and she'd never said a word.

In a sudden flash of memory, he could hear her voice telling Alicia, "I'd do *anything* for a good review."

Anything?

Like maybe seduce the reviewer? Like maybe pretend to be in love with him?

Webster's eyes moved to the date of the letter. In typical bureaucratic inefficiency, it had been sent weeks after his arrival date. Still, even if the mail was outrageously slow, Juliana had to have received this letter before they first made love.

Webster tossed the ring box down on Alicia's desk and went upstairs.

His head was spinning. He had to get out of here.

Juliana pulled the pickup truck into the Beckwiths' driveway, tapping her horn lightly. Chris and Jamey were playing in the empty garage, and they came running as she climbed out of the cab. Jamey started to launch herself at Juliana, then remembering her injured ribs, stopped and hugged her gently.

"What, no school today?" Juliana asked, kissing the top of Jamey's tangled hair and moving into the open garage, out of the rain.

"There's some kind of teacher's conference." Chris grinned. "That's just fine with me."

"Me, too," Jamey said.

"Lucky devils. Is your mom around?"

"She's lying down," Chris said. "She's not feeling real well, so I'm baby-sitting."

He put such an expression of long-suffering on his face Juliana had to laugh.

"I *don't* need a baby-sitter," Jamey said indignantly, opening her mouth to give him an additional piece of her mind. But Chris was quick to back down.

"Sorry, squirt," he said, his face sincere. "I keep forgetting that you don't need a sitter now that you're . . . five." And then he turned away from Jamey and dropped Juliana the best deadpan wink she'd ever seen. He was better at it than his father was, and that kind of wink was Sam Beckwith's trademark.

"Chris and I are doing a scientific experiment," Jamey told Juliana. "We're seeing who can fly the farthest, Barbie or Ken."

"We think that Ken will travel the longest distance, since he has the largest body weight," Chris said. "But we'll do a bunch of tests to make sure we're right."

"Well," Juliana said, unable to hide her smile. "Don't forget to take into consideration that Barbie is slightly more streamlined than Ken."

Chris nodded seriously. "We didn't think of that," he said.

"On the other hand," Juliana said. "Barbie's long hair might create more drag."

"My Barbie's bald," Jamey said. "I gave her a buzz cut last week."

Kids.

She'd never allowed herself to think about it before,

assuming that she'd be single all of her life, but she really, really wanted children. She wanted bright young faces, full of life and energy, full of laughter and an unquenchable need to discover the world.

She wanted Chris and Jamey, but they were already taken, so she'd have to make some beautiful children of her own. With Webster's help, of course. . .

Juliana smiled. The more she got used to this married thing, the more she liked it.

"Yo!" Liz called from the kitchen door. "You gonna stand out there all day?"

"See you later, guys," Juliana said, then went inside. "I thought you were lying down."

Liz made a face. "I tried, but as soon as I got comfortable, the baby started working on his new tap-dancing routine."

Liz looked tired, with signs of strain clearly showing on her face. "Will you look at those clouds?" she said, peering out of the kitchen window. "I really hope this rain doesn't change to snow."

"It's not cold enough," Juliana said.

"Yeah, you're right," Liz agreed. "I just worry whenever Sam's going to be driving late at night."

"He'll be fine," Juliana said.

"I have got the worst bitch of a backache today," Liz said, sitting at the kitchen table and resting her head on her arms. "Distract me, will you? Tell me about your romantic evening with Webster Donovan."

Juliana put some water in the tea kettle. "Don't you mean, my romantic evening with Webster and the Edgewoods?"

Liz sighed. "Oh, that's right. I forgot about the Edgewoods. They leave yet? They must've or you wouldn't be over here."

Juliana sat down across from Liz, pushing her hair back from her face. "Webster asked me to marry him."

Liz lit up, her pleasure erasing all of the lines of fatigue that had been on her face. "Congratulations!"

"I told him no."

"You're kidding?"

"No, but . . ." Juliana stood up to get the tea canister out of the cupboard. "I've changed my mind. I'm going to do it," she said. She looked at Liz, smiling a little self-consciously. "I'm going to marry him."

"All right!" Liz said, grinning. "Webster must be out of his mind, delirious with happiness."

"He, uh, doesn't know yet," Juliana said. "I haven't told him I changed my mind."

Liz stood up so fast that her chair fell over backwards. She pointed to the door. "Out!" she cried. "Get out! Get *out* of here and go tell that man what you just told me. Immediately!"

Laughing, Juliana let Liz push her out the door. "I'll call you later to see how you're feeling," she said.

"Go home!" Liz shouted. "Don't think about *me*, think about *Webster*!"

As Juliana climbed awkwardly into her truck, she could hear Liz singing the opening strains to the wedding march from the doorway.

She pulled onto the street and turned on the windshield wipers, noticing suddenly that the rain had traces of ice in it. Sleet, ugh, she thought. Still, it was too warm to freeze on the road. Or was it? The inside of the truck was so cold she put on the heater to warm her feet.

The firewood she'd picked up in town bounced in the back of the truck as she pulled into her driveway. Her ribs bounced, too, and she slowed, holding her side with one hand. It was enough to remind her that she wasn't back to normal yet. Heck, she wasn't even up to fifty percent. She wouldn't be able to unload the firewood. She'd have to ask Webster to do that for her.

By the time she parked the truck near the kitchen door, the rain had more than mere traces of ice in it.

It was positively chunky, and a few flakes were starting to fall. When she opened the door to the cab, the air was sharp and icy. Sweet heavens, the temperature was dropping fast.

The heels of her boots skidded slightly on the slippery driveway as she made her way into the house.

The kitchen was empty, but there was a mug out on the counter. Webster was awake.

Juliana hung her coat in the mud room and wiped her feet carefully on the mat, then went up the stairs to the second floor. The door to his room was open, and she approached it nervously.

What was she supposed to say? "Good morning, I changed my mind. Let's get married?"

There was a suitcase out and open on his bed, full of his clothes. He'd tossed them in there in obvious haste, as if getting away quickly was more important than having an entire wardrobe full of wrinkles.

She took another step into the room and then turned around, surprised, as Webster came in the door behind her. He was carrying the boxes for his computer, the ones he'd stored down in the basement. He stared at her, his eyes crystal blue.

"You're still upset," she said, taking a step back, away from the ice in his eyes.

"Very perceptive," he said, brushing past her, carrying the boxes into the sitting room.

His hair was wild, as it usually was, and he wore the jeans he'd had on when they'd first met. He'd washed them, but there were holes in the knees and the thighs were worn nearly white. He'd told her they were his traveling jeans.

She followed him into the other room. "Webster, I'm sorry—"

"Save it," he said, not even looking up.

"But—"

"Look, I found that letter, I know what your deal

is, so you don't have to play this game anymore," he said, his voice tight.

Juliana was lost. What on earth was he talking about? "Webster, I don't know what's going on," she said. "*What* letter?"

Webster glanced up from encasing his printer in Styrofoam packing material. He lowered it into the manufacturer's box. "Oh, we're going to play dumb? Fine. What letter? The one that's out on top of your desk."

She still looked at him blankly.

"In your office," he added. "The letter from the *Boston Globe*?"

Recognition flickered in her eyes, and Webster could have wept. Up to now, she'd been so convincingly confused he was starting to believe he'd made a mistake. But now it was clear that she knew which letter he was talking about.

He wound up his power cords and connecting cables and put them into the box with his computer keyboard.

"Webster, you're accusing me of something, and I have no idea what it is," Juliana said quietly. "I wish you would just come out and say it."

The blue eyes that looked at her were pure crystal, and Juliana felt the beginnings of real panic. This was not some misunderstanding or some mild disagreement. He was looking at her as if he couldn't stand the sight of her.

"You slept with me," he said. "You had sex with me not just once, but God almighty, I lost count of how many times. And you did it for one reason—because you knew that I was that damned reporter from the *Globe*, and you wanted a good review."

Juliana felt light-headed. Webster? Was from the *Boston Globe*? And sweet heavens! What he was accusing her of was little better than prostitution.

"Tell me, Jule," he asked, his eyes glittering. "Are you planning on making it an option for all the gentlemen guests? I can guarantee you'll increase your business that way, with or without a good review.''

The light-headedness was replaced by heat. Pure, unadulterated anger. How dare he? How *dare* he say such things?

"You are *so* wrong," she whispered. "I didn't know what was in that letter." She could prove it, but she wasn't going to bother. He wasn't worth the trouble. Her voice got stronger. "It's a good thing you're packing your bags, Mr. Donovan, because I want you out of my house."

Juliana moved toward the door, her head held high. She turned back, her face coolly, emotionlessly composed. "I'll expect you to stop in my office and settle your bill before you leave."

Webster finished packing, the silence of the room pressing down on him.

Outside, the rain was still coming down. And the temperature was plummeting, too. The driveway was a sheet of ice, so Juliana spread rock salt all the way down to the road. As she stood there in the rain, a snowplow drove slowly past. The plow was raised, but the big truck spread sand and salt across the road.

How could Webster have believed such terrible things about her? Even if he had thought those things, how could he have possibly said them out loud?

Why didn't he trust her? Why didn't he wait to talk to her before jumping to conclusions? If he had come to her and asked, she would have explained.

But it was too late. He'd ruined everything with his nasty, hurtful accusations. She'd never tell him now. Never.

Slowly she turned and went back to the house, grateful that the rain hid the tears on her face.

Webster finished loading his car, then went into the kitchen, stamping his boots on the mat. He swung open the door to the hallway and went into the office.

Juliana had laid all the paperwork out on Alicia's desk. "I've totaled up your phone calls and added that amount in," she said, her voice cool. "I've also totaled your meals separately from the room charge, in case you need that information for your expense account. Please feel free to check the math."

Her hair was swept up in a french braid, and she wore a black turtleneck shirt that contrasted her soft, pale skin. She kept her eyes carefully away from him, as if she couldn't bear to see him, even this one last time. Her eyelashes looked long and dark against her cheeks. God, she was so beautiful.

She felt him staring and glanced up. Her green eyes looked almost flat. All of the sparkle was gone as she looked at him coldly.

No, she didn't love him, Webster thought. That much was very clear. If she loved him, even just a little, he would've been able to see something in her eyes—maybe a little remorse.

Anger, deep burning anger flared inside him. He signed the credit-card slip, tucking his copy into his wallet, willing his hands not to shake. Taking out a crisp hundred-dollar bill, he dropped it on the desk in front of Juliana.

"Here's a little something extra," he said, his voice harsh, "since you obviously gave me VIP treatment."

If Webster wanted to see emotion in her eyes, he got it. He also got a stinging slap across the face. And he knew from the anger that suddenly seemed to radiate from her that if there hadn't been a desk between them, she would have used her knee and aimed a whole lot lower.

"Get out," she said, and he turned and left.

EIGHTEEN

Juliana hadn't felt this bad since the judge sentenced her to reform school, back when she was sixteen years old. As she was led out of the courtroom, she'd felt lost, doomed, and so desperate she could barely breathe.

She had that same feeling now.

If, if, if.

Her mind kept coming up with hindsight solutions, things she should have told him—hell—things *he* should have told *her*.

She wondered sadly if he would have been as quick to mistrust her if she had never been in trouble with the law.

Don't beat yourself up, she told herself sternly. Because that man was gone. And he wasn't coming back.

The doorbell rang.

Juliana glanced out of the window, wondering who on earth was out in this weather. The heavy rain had turned to thick snow about an hour ago, and four very solid looking inches had already fallen.

The Sheriff's four-wheel-drive Jeep sat out in front, chains on its wheels. Someone was in the passenger seat, but it was starting to get dark, and she couldn't see who it was.

She opened the front door and was hit by a blast of freezing air.

"Hey, Jule." Kurt grinned at her. He was wearing his arctic tundra gear, including a hat with earflaps that made him look about twelve years old. "How's it goin'?"

She opened the door wide so he could step into the entry hall. "What's the matter?" she asked, ignoring his question. "Is something wrong? Is it Liz?"

"Liz? Nah, she's fine," Kurt said. "I got a friend of yours out in my truck, though. He's got a temporary housing problem on account of this storm. See, we had to shut down the Pike, 'cause an eighteen-wheeler jackknifed. The driver's okay, and nobody else was hurt, thank the Lord, but there was an entire furniture showroom scattered for about a half a mile down the turnpike. Then reports started coming in that we had black ice on the pavement, so we decided to just keep the road closed.

"Local streets are fine," he continued, pulling off his hat and smoothing back his brown hair. "Provided you've got ice skates on your car instead of tires."

Juliana was giving him her overly patient look, which meant she wanted him to get to the point. "Turns out your buddy, Webster—"

"He's *not* my buddy," Juliana said threateningly.

"Fine," Kurt threw up his hands, backing up slightly. "But whatever you want to call him, the fact remains he drove his little red sports car off the road. I helped him pull it out of a ditch, but he then proceeded to travel in a sideways sort of manner down Route Seventy-three. I told Donovan that was definitely *not* the way Mr. Mazda intended that little car be driven, and I informed him that there was no way I was going to let him continue driving that vehicle with the current road conditions. Thanks to my incredibly persuasive debating techniques and my threat to fine him five hundred bucks if he continued to protest, I got him out of his car and into mine. And then——'' Kurt laughed, shaking his head in disbelief. ''This is what I really couldn't believe. . . .''

Juliana stood silently, arms crossed, waiting for him to continue.

''When I offered to drive him over here, Donovan told me that he wouldn't be welcome,'' Kurt said. ''Can you believe that? He wouldn't be welcome here at Benton's finest bed and breakfast?''

''He's not,'' Juliana said shortly.

Kurt studied her in mock amazement. ''*Not* welcome? I can't believe what I'm hearing,'' he said. ''I'd love to find out all the gory details, Jule, but I don't have time. I'm supposed to be out saving stranded motorists, not playing marriage counselor.''

''Watch it, Sheriff,'' Juliana said sharply. ''You're out of line.''

Kurt looked down at the floor. His wet boots were making puddles. ''Come on, Jule,'' he said quietly, all teasing set aside. ''Help me out, here. If Donovan can't stay with you, he's going to end up having to bunk down at the jail. And I don't know about you, but I wouldn't wish *that* on my worst enemy.''

Juliana swore a long string of very unladylike curses. Kurt politely didn't react. ''Tell him he can stay here,'' Juliana finally said, ''as long as he doesn't talk to me.''

Kurt leaned forward and gave her a kiss.

Through the snow-splattered windshield of the Jeep and the storm door of the house, Webster watched the handsome little sheriff wrap his arms around Juliana and kiss her not once, but twice. He wasn't prepared for the savage rush of jealousy that surged through him.

And he'd barely gotten it under control when the sheriff made his way back to the Jeep, slipping and sliding on the driveway. He came around to Webster's door and opened it.

"All clear," Kurt said cheerfully. "She's promised not to murder you in your sleep on the condition that you don't speak. At all."

"What if I refuse to get out of this car?" Webster asked. He was clutching his plastic carrying case of computer diskettes as if they were a life ring.

Kurt thought about that. "Well, then I'd have to lock you in jail until the weather got good enough to haul you over to the state psychiatric hospital, because obviously you'd be insane."

"You're the crazy one," Webster muttered, swinging his long legs out of the Jeep. "It's not normal for someone to be so goddamned happy all the time. I mean, doesn't it bother you that I've slept with your girlfriend?"

Kurt stopped midstride and stared back at Webster, surprise on his face. But then he laughed, one great big explosion of air and sound, and kept on walking up to the porch. He opened the door for Webster, gesturing grandly for him to enter the house.

He was nuts, thought Webster sourly. The man who was the county sheriff was absolutely bonkers.

The house was still and quiet, the only sound the big grandfather clock ticking. Webster put his diskettes on a table, then sat on a claw-footed chair and began pulling off his boots.

"Well," Kurt said blithely. "Looks like Juliana has gone into hiding. Tell her I'll give her a call as soon as the turnpike's open. Try not to kill each other— Oh, damn, I almost forgot. Wait a sec, I'll be right back."

He vanished out the door, but was back in only a few moments, carrying a bundle of letters in his hands.

"Got Juliana's mail," he said, stomping the snow off his boots before stepping inside. He handed the pile to Webster.

"Don't tell me," Webster said sourly. "You moonlight as the postman."

Kurt grinned. "Only when old Bob McFurley is on vacation," he said. "When's Alicia coming back? Soon?"

Webster shook his head. "No, not 'til Friday, I think."

"Some of those letters look important," Kurt said, zipping up his parka, and adjusting the earflaps on his hat. "You might want to check with Juliana, see if she wants you to read any of 'em to her."

"Read any of them to her?" Webster repeated, somewhat stupidly.

"Yeah." Kurt waved. "See ya later."

He pushed open the door, and went outside.

"Wait a minute!" Webster leapt up, following the sheriff out onto the porch in his stockinged feet. "Wait a minute. What do you mean, read them to her?"

Kurt turned and looked at the taller man, who was shivering in the freezing air. He laughed. "I don't believe she didn't tell you this," he said. "She didn't, did she?"

"Tell me what?"

"Never mind," Kurt said. "If she doesn't want you to know, *I* sure as hell don't want to be the one to tell you."

"Damn it, Pottersfield," Webster took a threatening step toward him. "If you don't tell me—"

But the sheriff didn't retreat. "My height's an illusion, pal," he said, a dangerous, almost crazy light in his hazel eyes. "You may think you can kick my ass, but I was a New York City cop for seven years, and I know all kinds of dirty tricks that will put you in the hospital, regardless of how tall you are. I'll also have the self-righteous pleasure of knowing that whether I win or lose, you'll end up in jail."

Webster stared at him. The smaller man was smiling

very slightly, looking as if he actually *wanted* Webster to try something stupid. And Webster was a pro at acting stupid. He had a sick feeling in the pit of his stomach that told him he may well have already acted stupidly enough for an entire lifetime.

"I'm sorry," he said. "Please. Just tell me. Why can't Juliana read her own mail?"

But Kurt shook his head. The dangerous look vanished quickly from his face, replaced by his carefree smile. "Sorry," he said, sounding not at all sorry. "You wanna know? Ask Jule. Oh, but that's a tough one, isn't it? She doesn't want you to talk."

Kurt started down the steps, then turned back. "Oh, yeah, I almost forgot. Tell Juliana that Amy said to say hi. Oops. But if you tell her, you'll be talking—"

"Amy?" Why couldn't Juliana read her own mail? "Who's Amy?"

Kurt grinned. "Amy. My wife. She's been working in Paris for the past two months."

Webster's toes were so numb he could barely feel them. The handsome little sheriff had a *wife*. He *wasn't* involved with Juliana . . . who couldn't read her own mail. . . .

"Well, if Juliana lets you do any talking, try to remember to mention that Amy'll be home a week from Friday. Tell Jule that she said she picked up a couple of really out-on-the-edge novels in London, and she's planning to put 'em on tape for her." Kurt grinned guilelessly. "Oops, I've given you another clue, haven't I?"

"You're a little bastard," Webster said, thoroughly frustrated. "Just tell me, goddamn it!"

"See ya," Kurt tossed the words over his shoulder as he slid back down to his Jeep.

"Juliana can't read, is that what you're trying to tell me?" Webster called after him.

But Kurt only waved merrily, the chains on his tires clanking as he pulled away.

Juliana didn't come out of her apartment until several hours after the power went off.

Webster had lit a fire in the bedroom that he'd used for so many weeks. He'd taken most of the wood that was in the shed to get it started, then sat there, hour after hour, staring into the flames.

Why couldn't Juliana read her own mail?

He'd had plenty of time to come up with theories, plenty of time to hypothesize, but he wouldn't find out the truth until he asked her.

But when Juliana appeared in the doorway, holding a candlestick in her hand, his mouth went dry and his mind blank.

Her hair was loose around her face, cascading down her back in a mass of red-gold curls that shimmered in the candlelight. Her eyes were distant, and she looked everywhere in the room but directly at him. She was wearing at least two sweaters under an overcoat. There were mittens on her hands and a scarf around her neck. The tip of her nose was pink, as if she was either very cold or had been crying.

"I'd appreciate it if you could help me carry some wood up to my apartment," she said stiffly.

It must have galled her to have to ask for help, Web realized. But with her broken ribs, she wouldn't be able to cart the heavy wood all the way up to the third floor.

"All right," he said quietly as he got to his feet.

He followed her down the stairs, her candle throwing out a small circle of light that seemed to surround them.

"Jule—" he started to say, but she cut him off.

"I don't want to talk to you," she said, her voice low.

"But Juliana—"

"*Please,*" she said, and he fell silent.

She waited while Webster pulled on his boots, then led him out onto the back porch.

"Woodshed's almost empty," he said quietly.

"There's a load of wood in the truck," Juliana said, refusing to meet his eyes. "It's already split. If you don't mind, you can bring some of that in, too."

The snow was still falling, thick and wet, and Webster went back inside to get his jacket.

Juliana set her candle on the porch, then grabbed a broom from the mud room and headed out to where the truck sat in the driveway. Nearly eight inches of heavy snow covered the wood that was in the truck bed.

But as soon as she stepped onto the driveway, her feet broke through the snow to the slick pavement below and then went out from underneath her. She grabbed wildly at the air, but there was nothing to hold on to, so she fell. The snow cushioned her fall, but not enough for her already injured ribs. Juliana felt a dizzying wave of pain engulf her, and she closed her eyes, hanging on, waiting for it to pass. Around her, the snow continued to fall, quietly, serenely.

Webster came back out on the porch and saw her sitting in the snow out by the truck.

"Are you okay?" he said, moving toward her quickly.

"Careful," she said. "It's—"

His feet hit the ice, and he slipped. He tried hard to get some traction, moving his legs furiously, like a cartoon character running in place. Gravity eventually won out, and he lost his balance and went down, landing on his rear end.

"—all ice," Juliana finished inadequately.

"Ouch," Webster said, a rueful grin on his handsome face. His look turned to concern. "Jule, did you hurt yourself?"

He already knew the answer to that question from the pain he could see in her eyes.

"I'm okay," she said tightly.

"Oh, God, don't start *that* again," Webster said, crawling toward her to help her up.

"Don't touch me," she said, backing away.

Webster rubbed his face tiredly with his hands. "Juliana, why would the Sheriff suggest that you might want me to read your mail to you?"

Juliana froze. Slowly she moved her head to look up into Webster's blue eyes. He knew. He knew, but he wasn't sure. And she didn't want to talk about it.

"Are you going to help me with the wood, or am I going to have to do it myself?" Using the truck's bumper for stability, Juliana painfully pulled herself to her feet. It was clear from her face that even that slight movement hurt her badly. Still she began sweeping the snow off the wood.

"I was wrong, wasn't I?" Webster said softly, standing up next to her and helping remove the snow. "You didn't know I was from the newspaper because you didn't read that letter. You *couldn't* read that letter."

"Oh, damn!" Juliana said. The wood had become one giant block, covered with a thick layer of ice that had frozen rock solid underneath the snow. It would have taken a strong man with a sledge hammer to break it apart, assuming that man could find someplace to stand without slipping and sliding. And even after the wood was freed from the ice, it would be wet and soggy and nowhere near ready to burn. "How much wood did you say was in the shed?" she asked Webster. Sweet heavens, her ribs hurt.

He looked down at her through the falling snow. Flakes had fallen on her hair, creating a shimmery veil of snow over her curls. She looked like an angel. How could he possibly have mistrusted her? He felt sick, remembering the things he had said and done in his anger. He reached out to brush a snowflake off her cheek, but was stopped by the hostility in her eyes.

He'd really blown it, he thought. She was never going to forgive him.

"There's probably enough wood to last through the night," Webster said. "Provided we share a fireplace."

Juliana swore, but weakly, with resignation. "My luck just never runs out, does it?" she said.

The firelight flickered across Juliana's face as she stared into the flames. If she was thinking at all about that other night they'd sat here in front of a fire, that first night they'd made love, her expression didn't give her away.

Webster watched her. "Jule," he said softly, and she looked up at him. He could still see the hurt in her eyes, and silently he berated himself. How could he have accused her the way he had? "You didn't read that letter, did you?"

She looked away from him, back toward the fire. When she spoke, her voice was low. "No."

"You can't read."

It wasn't a question, so she didn't bother to answer it. She just looked into the flames.

"I didn't know that," he finally said softly.

The firelike pain was back in her side every time she breathed in or out. It was appropriate, Juliana thought. As long as she was stuck here with Webster, it was fitting that she be in pain.

"Are you learning disabled?" he asked. "Dyslexic?"

This time it *was* a question, so she nodded. "Yes."

"Juliana," he said, "I honestly didn't know, and I'm sorry. I . . . I guess I kind of lost it, and I shouldn't have. I shouldn't've said those things to you."

"Damn right, you shouldn't have," she said, her green eyes sparking as she looked at him.

"I'm sorry," he said, ineffectively. "I'm really sorry—"

"Are you also sorry about not telling me that you were the reviewer?" Juliana asked sharply. "Funny, isn't it, Webster, that you got so angry at *me*, when all along it was *you* who weren't telling the truth. You should have told me you were from the newspaper right from the start."

"You should have told me you couldn't read," Webster countered.

"I was afraid to," Juliana said, her shoulders stiff. "I didn't think you'd understand."

"Yeah, well, join the club," Webster said. He stood up suddenly, stretching his long legs. He picked the candlestick up from the fireplace mantel and went to the door.

"Where are you going?" Juliana asked, curiosity getting the better of her.

"Up to your apartment," Webster said. "I'm going to get your ace bandage. That fall hurt you. Maybe if we wrap you up, you'll feel a little better."

"I'm okay," she protested.

"Yeah, right," Webster said. "I'll be back in a minute."

"My apartment's locked," she said tightly. "And I'm not giving you the key."

"I've still got my own key," Webster said, and disappeared into the darkness of the hallway.

Damn, thought Juliana, resting her head on her arms. Damn, damn, double damn! This was torture. It was going to take her long enough to get over him. She wanted him gone already. The sooner he left, the sooner she'd start healing.

Webster unlocked the door to Juliana's apartment and went inside, holding the candlestick in front of him. The apartment was hushed and dark, the skylights covered with thick, white snow. He moved slowly across the floor. If he were Juliana, he thought, where would he keep his ace bandages?

He opened the closet door. Rows of neatly hung clothing danced in the candlelight: all of Juliana's prim, high-necked blouses, the long skirts, the more brilliantly colored evening gowns. . . . Something sparkled, reflecting the candle's dim light and he stepped into the closet for a closer look. It was white, and it was a dress, and it was covered with literally thousands of tiny sequins. It looked tiny, as if it would barely fit a woman as tall as Juliana, but it was made with that spandex material, the stuff that was designed to tightly hug every female curve. Her legs would look a mile long in a dress this short, Webster thought, his knees suddenly weak.

He had to make her forgive him. He *had* to.

Backing out of the closet, Webster closed the door and held up his candle, looking around the room, peering in the dim light. The dresser, he thought. That was a good place to look.

The first drawer was underwear. There was an incredible selection—everything from cotton jockey briefs to delicate wisps of satin and lace. But no ace bandage. He was about to close the drawer and move on to the next when a piece of paper caught his eye.

It was the note he'd written and left for her down in her office. It was the note he'd written the morning after he first told her he loved her. It was the note that she couldn't read. And somehow he knew she hadn't let Alicia read it to her. He picked it up and slipped it into the back pocket of his jeans.

He pulled open the second drawer. It held Juliana's exercise clothes—and the ace bandage. Triumphantly, he gathered it up and started down the stairs.

Juliana didn't even look up when he came into the room.

"I found it," he said. He sat down next to her and warmed his hands, holding them out to the fire.

"If you think I'm going to let you put that thing on me, you're crazy," Juliana said quietly, still not looking up at him.

Webster studied her profile for a moment. He had to apologize. He had to make her understand. "Juliana, please, I am so sorry about what I said. You've got to forgive me."

"No, I don't," she said hotly, suddenly turning to face him.

His eyes were dark with misery. "No, you don't," he agreed. "But I'm asking you. Please, look at it from my perspective."

Juliana laughed humorlessly, then held her side from the pain. "You know what it looks like from your perspective?" she asked. "It looks like this is a damn convenient time for you to come crawling, asking for forgiveness. We're stuck here together, alone in this big house. Yeah, I'll bet you want me to forgive you, you son of a—"

"That's not fair."

"What do you want, Webster? You want to kiss and make up, right? And then what? Then you want me to take off my clothes so you can help me put on that ace bandage that you so gallantly went upstairs to fetch." Her voice dripped with sarcasm. "But, hey, as long as I've got my clothes off, you might as well take yours off, too. And then, who knows? Right, Webster?"

"No."

Tears of anger welled up in Juliana's eyes, and she blinked them furiously back. "Well, I hate to disappoint you," she said, "but I *did* hurt myself when I fell. Even if I were stupid enough to swallow your penitent crap, I wouldn't be able to give you what you want, not without it hurting. But you probably don't care."

He was watching her, his own eyes filled with tears. His face was full of pain, and his voice shook as he said, "I *do* care. I would never want to hurt you, Jule."

"You already did," she whispered. "I loved you, Webster, and you took that and you killed it. I can't forgive you. I don't think I ever will."

Webster felt sick. He *had* to make her understand. "Jule, when I saw that letter, it didn't occur to me that you didn't know what it said, that you couldn't read it. You've talked so many times about having 'read' one book or another that *honestly* I didn't know you can't read. Really, please, just tell me what I was supposed to think. Add to that the fact that you just turned down my marriage proposal. I was hurt. I was angry. I—"

"That doesn't excuse the things you said to me," Juliana said.

"No," Webster said quietly. "You're right. It doesn't excuse what I said and did. But maybe it can make you understand how I was feeling. And maybe if you understand that, you'll be able to forgive me."

Juliana stared into the fire. "I'm sorry," she said, her voice barely more than a whisper. "I can't."

NINETEEN

Webster awoke from a dreamless sleep with a rough hand shaking his shoulder. The fire had dwindled to little more than glowing embers, and the room was cold. He stared up into a small, frightened face and then was hit by the beam of a flashlight.

He swore, closing his eyes against the brightness. When he dared to open his eyes again, the little face, which was attached to a small, wiry body wrapped in a bright-yellow snowsuit, had knelt down next to Juliana.

"Chris!" he heard her exclaim. She groaned softly as she sat up, unable to cover the aching pain he knew she was feeling from her re-injured ribs.

"Jule, it's Mommy," a small, scared voice said. "She's gonna have the baby, and Daddy's not home. Phone's out, too. You gotta come quick."

"Oh, my Lord," Juliana exclaimed. "You came all this way in the dark by yourself?"

Chris nodded. His eyes held a determination that made him seem a good ten years older than he was. "I didn't have a choice."

Webster was already on his feet, pulling his boots

on, shrugging into his leather jacket. He lit the candle, and it threw dim light into the room.

"Chris," he said. "Run down to the mud room and see if you can find me a pair of gloves or mittens— anything like that, okay? And gather up Juliana's jacket and hat."

"But—"

"Go on, Chris," Juliana said, smiling at the little boy. "Webster's got to help me wrap up my broken ribs. We'll be down in one minute. I promise."

He nodded and left.

Juliana was still wearing her big overcoat, and she slid it awkwardly off her shoulders. Her whole body had stiffened up while she slept, and she couldn't pull her sweater up over her head. "Webster, help me," she said, and then he was next to her, pulling off first one sweater, then the other, then the long thermal undershirt she had underneath it all.

She wasn't wearing a bra, and her nipples stood erect in the cold air, teasing his eyes. Webster tried hard to ignore that fact as he gently wound the ace bandage around her lower ribs. But it was like that old saying, the best way to think about an elephant is to try not to think about an elephant. . . .

His hand brushed the soft underside of her breast. "Sorry," he whispered, glancing up at her. For an instant, he thought he saw a remnant of her desire for him spark in her eyes. Maybe the cold wasn't the only thing her body was reacting to.

"Juliana, I think you're the most beautiful woman in the world," he said, his voice husky.

"Just hurry," she said, not meeting his eyes again.

He fastened the little metal clasps, and helped slip her shirt back on. "What's the fastest way to the Beckwiths'?" he asked, helping with her sweaters.

"Depends," Juliana said. "Do you think the road's still all ice?"

Webster followed her down the stairs. Chris was waiting at the bottom, holding her jacket and hat.

"I cut across the field," Chris said, wiping his nose on the back of his hand. "Snow's pretty deep, but when I tried walking on the road, I kept slipping. They haven't even plowed yet. I don't think they can. Up the road, I could see a snowplow that skidded into the trees."

"Oh great. And I don't even have chains on my tires," Juliana said, leading the way into the mud room. "But I *do* have snowshoes." She pointed up to where a variety of webbed snowshoes hung on the wall. Webster reached up, unhooking two large pairs and one smaller pair.

"Grab the backpack, too, Web," Juliana said. "Do me a favor and go out to the truck and pull my CB radio out of the dash. We can hook it up to Liz's car and at least try to call for some help."

In a matter of moments, they were heading out across the field. The snow had changed back to a fine, light rain. It was still cold enough to freeze, and the snow covering the ground and all the trees was glazed with a thin film of ice. Everything sparkled in the light from Chris's flashlight. If they had been out for a pleasant stroll, it would've been breathtakingly beautiful.

"Keep your legs spread," Juliana called to Chris and Webster. "Or you'll end up tripping over your own feet."

Walking with the snowshoes on was grueling, and Juliana's side throbbed relentlessly. But she pushed herself harder, faster, thinking about Liz, alone in the house with a five-year-old, about to give birth.

"Jule." Webster was next to her, striding along effortlessly. "I'm going to run ahead," he said, his voice pitched low, so the boy behind them couldn't hear. "Slow down a bit, so Chris can keep up."

And so you don't die of pain before you get there.

He didn't say the words, but Juliana could see in his eyes that he was concerned about her. She nodded, and he picked up his pace, pulling ahead and quickly disappearing into the darkness.

"Come on, Chris," Juliana said. "We're almost halfway there."

Webster slipped the snowshoes off and went in through the kitchen door. He put the backpack on the counter.

"Liz?"

"In here," she called. "Is Chris with you? Is Chris all right?"

"He's fine. He's with Juliana. They'll be here in a few minutes," Webster said, following Liz's voice into the bedroom. Candles were everywhere, and shadows danced on the walls. The air in the room was chill, despite a fire that burned in the fireplace. Liz lay in the middle of a king-sized bed, with little Jamey next to her, fast asleep.

Liz swore as a contraction gripped her. Despite the cold, sweat stood out on her forehead, and her body tensed. "Lord, they're coming faster now," she moaned. "I wasn't ready for this one—"

"Hold my hand," Webster commanded, sitting next to her on the bed. "Look at me, Liz. And breathe. Did you take Lamaze?"

"Hell yes," Liz gasped, panting hard, as if she was trying to exhale all the pain.

Finally the contraction ended, and she lay back, exhausted. Two small tears trailed down her cheeks from the corner of her eyes. "My Lamaze instructor forgot to tell me how to stay relaxed when I went into labor in the middle of an ice storm, with my husband God knows where," she said. "Congratulations, by the way."

Webster looked at her blankly. Congratulations for

what? She already knew he finished the first draft of his book.

"Jule told me you popped the big question." Liz smiled weakly. "She told me she said no at first, but that she changed her mind, that she wanted to marry you—"

Another contraction hit, and Liz's fingers squeezed Webster's. "Breathe," he said. "Keep breathing," but he wasn't sure if he was reminding Liz or himself.

Juliana had told Liz that she wanted to marry him. *Had* wanted. Past tense. God almighty—Juliana had come home to tell him that, and he'd accused her of those terrible things. He'd really, truly blown it.

Liz's contraction seemed to last forever, and when it finally relented, she curled up on her side, her face buried in her pillow so her daughter wouldn't hear her sobs. "I want Sam," Webster heard her say. "I want to know that he's safe, not driving around in this weather or lying in some ditch somewhere."

"Liz, we brought over Jule's CB radio, and as soon as she gets here, I'll try to track him down," Webster said.

Liz dried her face on the flannel sheet, hope in her eyes. "Do you think you can?"

Webster smiled. "He's probably as anxious for news of you as you are for news of him. He shouldn't be too hard to find."

"I just want to know that he's safe," Liz said again.

"Mommy!" Chris ran into the room, and Liz held out her arms to her son. He hugged her fiercely.

"I'm so proud of you," she whispered, stroking his hair. "So proud."

Webster looked up as he felt Juliana's hand on his shoulder. As he met her eyes, he felt jarred, devastated by the knowledge that she might've been his forever. She *would* have been his . . . if he hadn't gone and opened his big, stupid mouth. She should've been his, but she wasn't, and the fault was only his own.

Her green eyes watched him steadily in the candle-light, her beautiful mouth unsmiling, her cheeks paler than they should be after a brisk walk in the cold air—pale from the pain of her broken ribs. He ached to pull her into his arms.

"Why don't you get Chris and Jamey set up in one of the other rooms. Get a fire going," she said quietly.

"Shouldn't I do something like . . . you know . . . boil water?" he asked. "That's what they always do in the movies—except I'm not sure why."

Juliana smiled, real warmth in her eyes. Webster felt his heart pound. Maybe there was hope for them. "I'll need some string and a pair of scissors," she said, "to cut the umbilical cord. You need to boil the water to sterilize them."

Webster nodded. "At last," he said, "one of the great mysteries of life cleared up." He stood up. "Come on, Chris. I need you to find me a pair of scissors, some string, and a sleeping bag or some blankets to put on the floor for your sister."

He scooped the sleeping Jamey up in his arms and left the room, talking easily to Chris the entire time.

Liz smiled weakly up at Juliana. "He's going to be a good father," she said.

Juliana couldn't meet her friend's eyes. "How far apart are your contractions?" she asked.

"I don't know," Liz said. "Around five minutes. But the last few were a lot less, like maybe only three minutes apart. I'm going to have this baby at home, aren't I?"

Juliana nodded. "I'm afraid so."

Liz took a deep breath, blowing the air out hard. "Well," she said. "I always hated being in the hospital. I just want to know where Sam is."

*   *   *

Webster finished attaching Juliana's CB radio to Liz's Jeep, then pulled out of the garage into the driveway. The tires slid as soon as they hit the ice, and the Jeep came to rest against a row of snow-covered bushes. Chris sat quietly beside him, his brown eyes round.

Web flipped immediately to channel nine. "I've got an emergency," he said, pressing the talk switch on the microphone. "Is anyone listening?"

He released the button, adjusting the squelch control.

"You've reached the police station," came a tired female voice. "Go ahead."

"I'm over at the Beckwith place," Webster said into the mike. "Liz Beckwith's gone into labor. We're looking for medical assistance, and we're trying to find the whereabouts of her husband, Sam Beckwith."

"This is Kurt Pottersfield," came the Sheriff's voice. "This Webster?"

"Yeah."

"Look, I'm on my way," Kurt said. "I've got a snowmobile. I'll stop and pick up Doc Rogers. I should be there within an hour."

Webster glanced at his watch. If Juliana had been right when he'd gone in to check on Liz after sterilizing the scissors, they didn't have an hour. "Right now all Liz wants to know is whether or not Sam is safe. Can you help us find him? I've got to get back inside, but Chris is here."

"Chris?" a female voice emerged scratchily from the static. "I'm Louise, remember me?"

Webster handed the mike to Chris, and opened the car door.

"Yes, ma'am," Chris said.

"I'm going to radio the state police, see if they can help locate your dad, okay? So hold on."

Webster skidded on the ice, sliding his way back inside the house. In the living room, Jamey was sleeping peacefully in front of the glowing fireplace. He checked to make sure the screen would keep any stray sparks from escaping, then went down the hall toward the bedroom.

Liz was crying softly. Juliana glanced up at him, shaking her head. "I think she's in transition," she murmured, "and she's wearing herself out. She's convinced Sam's been in some horrible car accident, and that she's never going to see him again. She's using up all the energy she's going to need to deliver this baby."

"She loves him," Webster said softly. "She's afraid of being without him. I can relate."

His face was so serious, his eyes so blue, so open that she felt she could see deep into his soul. He loved her. He wanted her to forgive him. Juliana could see it every time she looked at him.

Liz cried out as another contraction started, and Juliana pulled her eyes away from his.

"Breathe, Liz. Come on," Juliana said. "Focus! Come on, Liz. Keep your eyes open. Look at me!"

"How can I help?" Webster asked.

"Find Sam!" Juliana said.

Webster turned, running down the hall, back toward the kitchen door. His eyes fell on a boom box that was sitting on the counter by the stove. A quick inspection told him it was plugged into the wall, but it also had batteries inside. He switched over to direct current, and turned it on. Music. The batteries were low, but if he pushed up the volume, the radio worked. And it played country music from WCNT out of Springfield.

Webster turned it off to conserve the batteries, then went outside to the Jeep.

"Any luck?" he asked Chris.

The boy shook his head. "They're trying to track down the guy who organized the benefit concert last night," he said, "to see if he knows where my dad is."

Web climbed into the driver's seat and took the microphone from Chris. "I got an idea," he said, and keyed the talk switch. "Louise?"

"I'm still here," she said. "Who's this?"

"Webster Donovan. Look it, do they have telephone service in Springfield? How bad did the storm hit out there?"

The radio crackled. "Not as bad as out here. State police report roads are still solid ice, though. As for the phones, I think it depends on whether or not trees and lines are down. Why?"

"Do me a favor and radio the Springfield police. If they've got their phones working, ask them to call WCNT—"

The radio squealed horribly and Webster nearly dropped the mike.

"Sorry 'bout that," Louise said. "But I had to break in. They've found Sam. He's snowed in at a rest stop on the Pike. The man's damn near going out of his mind, worrying about Liz."

Webster grinned at Chris, holding up a high five for the boy to slap. "All right! We found him!" He keyed the mike. "Tell Sam to get on the phone and call WCNT. . . ."

Juliana looked up as Webster came back into the room. He was carrying the boom box from the kitchen, and he set it down on the bedside table. He turned it on and adjusted the antennae. Trisha Yearwood was singing about living on the wrong side of Memphis. Webster turned the volume up.

"Webster—" Juliana started.

"Shh," he said. "Listen. Liz, are you listening?"

Liz looked smaller than ever, her usually cheery face pale and streaked with tears, her eyes listless.

The song cut off midchord, as the DJ's voice interrupted. "Lot of people out there have lost their power and the phones tonight, and I've got a caller on the line who's real anxious to talk to his wife—''

"Liz, honey, it's me.''

Liz looked sharply up at Webster. Sam. It was Sam's voice. On the radio. He was safe. He was alive.

"Damn it, Liz,'' Sam's voice broke. "I wish to hell I could hold you in my arms right now, but I can't. You got to hold Juliana's hand instead—and listen to her. Breathe like she tells you to. Promise me you will?''

"I promise,'' Liz whispered, her eyes filled with tears. "Oh, Jule, he's okay—''

"I love you, Liz,'' Sam said, his voice thick with emotion. "I'll always regret that I wasn't there for you when Chris was born. And I wish that I could be there to hold this new child in my arms as he takes his first breath. But even though my body isn't with you, honey, my heart is. And if you close your eyes, you can feel my love around you—'' His voice broke again, but Liz could hear laughter along with Sam's tears. "Damn it, girl, we don't do too well with timing, do we?''

The DJ's voice came in. "We got Sam Beckwith on the phone, going out live to his wife Liz, who's having her baby at home tonight on account of this storm. Hang on, Liz. We got all our listeners pulling for you. We're going to play only your husband's songs 'til we get the word you've had the baby.''

Music started and Sam's familiar voice began to sing one of the many love songs he'd written for Liz.

Juliana looked up at Webster. There were tears on his face, she realized with shock. He turned away from her, unable to meet her eyes.

He could have had a love like Sam's, he thought. He could've watched Juliana walk smiling down the aisle of a church, eager to spend the rest of her life with him. He could've had a love that ignored all boundaries of time and place, a love that he could have spoken of openly, even in front of thousands of listeners over the radio airways, the way Sam did. He could've had Juliana.

But he blew it.

He stood up to leave the room, but Liz's soft voice stopped him. "Webster, thank you."

He nodded, afraid to talk for fear of loosening the flood of emotions inside him.

He wanted to run outside into the night to cry until he was numb, but he didn't. He couldn't. He had to be on hand for when Juliana needed him. So he pushed it all back down inside and went into the kitchen and boiled some more water on the gas stove—this time to make some coffee.

It wasn't more than ten minutes later when Juliana called him back into the bedroom. "She's crowning," Juliana said softly. "Go wash your hands and take off your jacket and shirts. Put on one of Sam's T-shirts. They're in the dresser."

"Second drawer from the top," Liz said between gasps for air. She swore loudly. "Christ, Jule, I gotta push."

Webster scrambled for the bathroom, quickly stripping off everything but his jeans and boots. He washed carefully, drying himself on a clean towel from the linen closet.

"Get a clean shirt out for me, too," Juliana called to him.

He slipped a T-shirt on, carrying another toward the bed.

Liz was between contractions, her legs up, knees bent. Her hair was soaked with perspiration, and sweat dripped from her face. The top of the baby's head was clearly visible between her legs.

Juliana awkwardly began shedding layers of sweaters. Webster helped her, pulling off her long-sleeved undershirt, then pulling on the clean T-shirt. The thin white cotton was nearly transparent, but there wasn't enough time for him to be distracted.

Another contraction started.

"I've got to push," Liz announced, "and you can go to hell if you don't want me to, because I'm gonna!"

"Go for it," Juliana said, helping Liz up into a better position.

Liz pushed, shouting with exertion.

"God almighty," Webster breathed, watching the baby's head emerge from Liz's body.

"Support the baby's head!" Juliana said.

"Me?" But even as he asked, he reached out, holding the tiny little head in his fingers. It was warm, hot almost, and it moved, the tiny face grimacing. God almighty, it was alive!

Liz took a deep breath, ready for the next contraction.

"Are you okay?" Juliana asked him, and he nodded.

To his shock, Webster didn't want to let go of the baby. It was warm and mushy, slimy as hell, but he didn't want to let it go. He wanted to hold this tiny little new life in his hands. He wanted to catch it as it entered the world, be the first representative of the human race to welcome it to life.

Juliana smiled at him, as if she understood, and took Liz's hand.

"One more big push," she said. "The baby's head's out—the worst's over. Come on, Liz, you've done this before."

On the radio, Sam spoke, still standing at the pay phone at some rest stop along the Massachusetts Turnpike. His voice was low and soothing, sounding intimate as he spoke to his wife across the miles, through the airwaves. No matter that thousands of people were listening in, no matter that the radio station was surely taping the broadcast for future use. This was the only way he could get close to Liz right now when she needed him. And that was all that mattered.

The DJ segued into Sam's current release, and Liz braced herself as another contraction started. She pushed, holding tightly to Juliana's fingers, and the baby slid out into Webster's waiting hands.

"It's a boy," he whispered.

"Clear his nose and mouth," Liz gasped, and Juliana reached out with her fingers and gently wiped the baby's nose and mouth clean. The infant took one deep, shuddering breath and began to cry.

"Well," Dr. Rogers said from the doorway, where he stood with Kurt and Chris. "Looks like you did just fine without me."

"It's a boy," Webster said again, laughing through a blur of tears as he looked down at the tiny new life in his hands. "Chris, get on that radio and get the news to your dad. He's got himself another son!"

_____ TWENTY _____

Juliana went tiredly into the kitchen and poured herself a cup of the coffee that Webster had made. He was sitting at the table, and she could feel his eyes on her. Dawn had come hours ago, and as the sky got lighter, the temperature had started to rise. The rain kept falling, but now it melted the snow and ice. In another few hours, the plows would get through, and the roads would be cleared.

"That was the most amazing thing I've ever been a part of in my entire life," Webster said, his voice low and husky.

She walked to the table and sat down across from him. "Yeah," she said. "Me, too."

She was still wearing only the T-shirt he'd gotten her from Sam's drawer, and she shivered in the cold air. The thin cotton shirt *was* transparent, Webster realized. He could see her breasts as clearly as if she were wearing a diaphanous nightgown.

Webster felt the familiar tightening in his groin. God almighty, he would never get enough of her, would he? And the twenty-million-dollar question was whether she still expected him to get up and drive away from her after they'd shared this miracle.

"I was really impressed that you thought of putting Sam on the radio as a way for him to talk to Liz," Juliana said.

Webster shrugged. "It was nothing—"

"It was *everything* to Liz," Juliana said, "and you know it."

"Yeah, I do know," he admitted. "I'm just . . . really glad I could help."

"You did help," Juliana said quietly. "And I'm glad you were here."

"Juliana—" he started to say.

But she shook her head and didn't let him speak. She walked out of the room before he could say another word.

It wasn't quite eleven o'clock in the morning when the sound of a helicopter drummed over the house. The big chopper headed for the field between the Beckwiths' house and Juliana's, and the doors opened almost before it set down.

Sam Beckwith was out, running across the field toward the house, slipping and sliding in the snow. Jamey and Chris met him halfway, and they all collapsed in one big pile of arms and legs, laughing and giddy.

Sam gave each of his children a kiss, then scrambled free, heading for the house—and Liz.

Juliana was in the bedroom with Liz when Sam appeared. He just stood there, watching his wife breastfeed his infant son. The big man's dark eyes filled with tears as he looked into Liz's smiling face. Juliana slipped out of the room, closing the door gently behind her.

Kurt was in the kitchen, leaning against the counter, the earflaps of his hat raised, making him look more like a cartoon character than a county sheriff. Dr. Rogers wound his scarf about his neck as he poured himself another cup of coffee. Webster just sat at the table, staring at Juliana, still wearing only a short-sleeved T-shirt, as if he weren't affected by the cold.

She pulled her jacket more tightly around her, carrying her sweaters and long-sleeved shirt. Her ribs ached so much she couldn't pull them on by herself.

As if reading her mind, Webster cleared his throat. "Let me help you," he said softly.

She stared at him a moment, her green eyes wide.

What does she see? Webster wondered. He hoped with all his heart she saw a man worthy of a second chance, a man who loved her, heart and soul.

"No thanks," she murmured.

Webster turned away, hiding the disappointment that he knew showed clearly in his eyes. She didn't want his help. She'd accepted it for a while when the stakes were high, but now she didn't need him anymore.

"Come on, Webster," Kurt said cheerfully. "The roads are clear—they've reopened the Pike. I'll give you a lift to your little car."

"Just make sure he doesn't give you a ride on that snowmobile of his," Dr. Rogers said, rolling his eyes. "Aged me thirty years, that did."

"You loved it, you old liar," Kurt said. "I heard you whooping and hollering."

"That was fear, son," the older man said. "You get to be my age, and you don't walk away from falling off one of those contraptions, going thirty miles an hour."

"Oh, what are you? Fifty? That's not old," Kurt scoffed. He continued to tease the doctor, but Webster stopped paying attention. Juliana had wandered out of the house, and she stood now in the driveway.

The rain had stopped, and a gentle wind blew, moving her red-gold hair. With the temperature continuing to climb, everything was dripping—the trees, the roof, the bushes.

Webster pulled on his sweater and his leather jacket and pushed open the kitchen door. He went and stood behind Juliana on the driveway, waiting for her to turn around, but she didn't move.

He took another step toward her, and she spoke. "I guess this is good-bye for us." She did turn, then, and her eyes were cool, detached—Miss Anderson's eyes, not Juliana's.

Webster just looked at her. With extreme clarity, he could remember the way that soft, moist baby had felt in his hands. He had felt the infant shudder as he took in his first deep breath of air. That child he'd held had just been born. That baby was a new life, tiny and perfect, with no past mistakes and no regrets.

Webster wanted to be able to make as fresh a start. He didn't want to say good-bye, he wanted to say hello, to start over. He would say, "Hi, I'm Webster Donovan, from the Boston Globe," and she would say, "My name is Juliana Anderson, and I'm dyslexic," and there would be no room for misunderstandings.

She was still looking at him, waiting for him to say something. So he said something.

"No."

There was surprise in her eyes now, but Webster didn't say anything else.

He just stood there, remembering the sound of Sam's deep voice talking to Liz over the radio. The country singer had been unconcerned with how he sounded to anyone but his wife, unafraid of letting the entire world know how much he loved her. His love gave him strength and purpose.

Sam would never let Liz get away from him.

"No," Webster said again. "I'm not leaving town."

"What?"

"You heard me," he said. "I'm not gonna go. I'm

in love with you, Juliana, and I'm going to marry you.''

Juliana's eyes flashed. ''Forced marriages are frowned upon in this state.''

Webster shrugged. ''I'm not going to force you. You can say no. But I'll just keep hanging around until you change your mind.''

His blue eyes held crystal determination as he looked at her steadily. Juliana crossed her arms and laughed without humor at his audacity. ''And what makes you think I'd even agree to let you 'hang around?' ''

''Eternal hope,'' Webster said.

''Well, forget it,'' Juliana said. ''It's never going to happen.''

Webster shrugged again. ''So I'll get an apartment in town. And *then* I'll just keep coming by until you change your mind.''

''That's . . . ridiculous.''

''No, it's not,'' Webster said. ''Every day, I'll come to see you, and I'll tell you that I love you, and I'll beg you to forgive me, and I'll ask you to marry me. Sooner or later, you'll believe me, and sooner or later, you'll give in. So you might as well make it easier on yourself and tell me that you'll marry me right now.''

She turned away from him. ''Just go back to Boston, Webster.''

He stepped toward her, close enough to brush a wayward curl from her face. ''I can't do that, Jule,'' he said gently.

She pulled away from him. ''And I can't forgive you.''

Webster smiled, suddenly. ''You have to. You promised me you would.''

Juliana sighed. ''Webster, please—''

But he was pulling something out of the back pocket of his jeans. ''When I went into your apartment to get your ace bandage,'' he said, ''I found this.''

It was the letter he'd written to her, the morning after he had first told her that he loved her. "Did you get Alicia to read this to you?" he asked.

She shook her head. "No."

" 'Bout time you heard what I wrote, don't you think?"

"No, Webster—"

"Dear Juliana," Webster read. "Words are my tools, my trade, yet my mind is blank as I try to express all that I'm feeling in my heart. I love you. I've never written those words to another person before. I've certainly never had these feelings before. The strength and power of what is in my heart scares me to death. I want all of you, all at once, all the time. It's more than wanting you physically, though, God almighty, I can't think about you without getting hard. Still, when we make love, I'm fulfilled in ways I've never even imagined, ways that go beyond sexuality.

"Juliana, my love for you is endless and overpowering, and it's so new to me. I only ask one thing of you. If you accept my love, you must also be prepared to forgive me for all the mistakes I'll probably make. Please remember that if I act crazy, if I lose control, it's only because I love you so much.

"And I signed it, 'Yours always, Webster.' "

She laughed, looking up at him, and shaking her head. "You are *such* a jerk. You're making that up."

"No, I'm not." Webster took a step closer to her. She was weakening, he could tell by the light in her eyes. *Please God,* he prayed, *don't let me mess this up.* "Say you'll marry me, and I'll read you the first draft of my book."

She laughed again. "Yeah, and you'll make *that* up as you go along, too."

Webster grabbed her wrist and pressed the letter into her hand. "Go inside," he urged her. "Have Kurt or Dr. Rogers read it to you."

"You think I won't," she said. "You think I'll be too embarrassed."

Webster smiled, his eyes an odd mixture of crystal and soft blue. "If it does say those things I just said, will you marry me?"

Juliana snorted. "Oh, come on, Webster. I play poker, too. You're trying to bluff me. Well, I'm calling your bluff."

She turned to go inside. Webster leaned against the Jeep.

"Aren't you coming with me?" she asked, turning back to look at him. He looked so calm and relaxed, his long, muscular legs stretched out in front of him, crossed at the ankles, his hands casually tucked in the front pockets of his jeans. He had a small smile on his face, and his thick dark hair tumbled over his forehead.

She jammed her own hands in the pocket of her jacket, forcing her eyes down to the beat-up toes of his boots. Damn this man for being able to look so gorgeous when she was trying to be angry at him . . .

He shook his head. "I'll wait out here." This was one work he'd prefer not to hear read in front of an audience.

She turned, a flash of red-gold, and went in the kitchen door.

Webster stood, kicking at the chunks of ice still on the driveway for a long, long time. For a man who didn't consider himself very religious, he was spending an awful lot of time praying lately, he thought. He closed his eyes, letting his head tip back against the Jeep. He was going to win this one, he knew, because he loved her. Even if it didn't happen today it would happen another day. He loved her, and he knew that she still loved him. He *knew* it. . . .

Finally, *finally*, Juliana came back out of the house.

She stood in front of him, looking at him. "I was so mad at you," she said. "You jerk."

Was.

Webster straightened up. "Do you forgive me?" he asked, not daring to touch her. But his hands came out of his pockets, ready to reach for her, as if they had a mind of their own.

Juliana looked down at the letter she still held in her hands. "I have to," she said. "Don't I?"

Webster did reach out then, cupping her chin with his hand, pulling her face so that she had to look at him. "No, you don't have to," he said quietly.

"Yes, I do," she said just as quietly, meeting his gaze steadily. "It's like you said in your letter. If I want the sweet man who loves me, I've got to be prepared to put up with the jerk."

Webster winced. "You're taking liberties with your paraphrasing," he said, "but I guess that's essentially what I said."

They were both silent for a moment. Webster looked down at Juliana until she met his eyes. "Jule, will you take me back?" he asked, hardly daring to breathe.

As he watched, her eyes filled with tears. One escaped down her cheek, and she didn't try to brush it away. Another fell, another and another. She was crying. Juliana, who only cried for death or the equivalent, was crying.

"Yes," she whispered.

As he looked at her, he could see through the tears to the love in her eyes. She loved him. He was so happy he almost broke down and cried, too. Almost.

Instead, he leaned forward. His mouth brushed hers gently, and she felt him sigh before he kissed her again, harder this time. She melted against him, tasting coffee and the sweet taste that was so distinctly Webster.

From the kitchen door, Kurt, Sam, and Dr. Rogers stamped, applauded, and hooted.

Webster opened his eyes slowly to look at Juliana.

"How many of them were in the room when my

letter was read?'' he asked, bracing himself for the worst.

"All of them."

He nodded, then kissed her again, ignoring the catcalls and hubba-hubbas coming from the kitchen door. Strangely enough, he didn't care. They could tease all they wanted, but he didn't even care.

"Marry me," he said, catching one of her tears with his finger.

"You don't care that I can't read?" Juliana asked softly.

He gave her a look that said she had to be kidding. She gave him his answer in the form of a kiss.

Inside the house, Chris's clear voice rang out, "Mom says if you don't stop bothering Juliana and Webster, you're all gonna be in *big* trouble."

Webster waved to Kurt, then closed the big front door as the Jeep pulled back down the driveway. Juliana had already tiredly climbed up the stairs, so he went into the sitting room and grabbed a bottle of brandy from the sideboard.

The power had come back on, and the furnace was thudding quietly in the basement, sending warmth through the radiators.

Warmth. Webster wanted to feel warm. He wanted to take a warm shower and climb into a warm bed and sleep for two straight days. Well, maybe not sleep *right* away. . . .

He went up the stairs, stopping uncertainly on the second floor, looking into the room that had been his bedroom for so many weeks.

But Juliana wasn't in there.

Slowly he went to the foot of the stairs leading to Juliana's apartment. Slowly, he dared to look up.

The door was open.

She'd left the door open for him.

All of his final doubts vanished. She wanted him to come upstairs. She wanted to share her life with him.

Webster stopped moving slowly then, as he took the stairs two at a time. He went through the door and closed it tightly behind him.

He could hear the sound of water running. The Jacuzzi, he thought, and more than his tired muscles approved.

The bathroom door was open, and he stood in the doorway, watching Juliana pull off her boots and her socks. She smiled at him and took the bottle of brandy from his hand, setting it on the edge of the big tub.

Steam was starting to fog up the edges of the big mirrors, and Webster closed the door, keeping the warmth inside the room.

Juliana watched him in the mirror as she brushed out her hair. She let her eyes trail down the length of him, lingering on the tight bulge in his pants that gave away his desire for her.

"That happens just from *thinking* about me?" she said, her eyebrows raised.

"All the time," he said huskily, crossing toward her. "Constantly. You don't even have to be in the room." He pulled her toward him, fitting her hips tightly against his. "And if you are in the room, it's relentless."

She kissed him, letting her tongue trail lightly across his lips. "That's nice to know," she said.

He pulled off her sweater, then stopped as his fingers felt her ace bandage through the thin fabric of her shirt. "I don't want to hurt you," he said, frowning. "Maybe we should wait."

She stepped out of her jeans and took off the T-shirt. "Help me, will you?" she asked, motioning to the metal clasps that secured the elastic bandage.

Gently, he unfastened them and unwound the bandage. The bruise on her ribs was a rainbow of colors.

It hurt him just to look at it as she stood naked in front of him.

Her hands found the button at the top of his pants, but he took a step backward. "Jule, I'm serious," he said. "We can wait. We've got the rest of our lives, right?"

Juliana reached out and took his hand, turning it over and touching his palm lightly with her fingers. "These hands were gentle enough to help bring a baby into the world, Web. I'm willing to bet you can make love to me without hurting me."

He cupped her face with his hand, losing himself in her greenish eyes. "I love you," he whispered.

"Tell me the truth," she whispered back, unbuttoning his pants and pushing them down off his smooth, sleek body. "That wasn't the *real* letter you wrote to me, was it?"

Webster smiled, kicking his legs free. He stepped into the Jacuzzi, holding out his hand for her.

"Aren't you going to answer my question?" she asked, sitting down next to him in the warm, bubbling water.

"What question?" Webster asked as he gently pulled her onto his lap and kissed her. With a sigh, she ran her fingers through his dark, curly hair.

And in a matter of a few short seconds, she forgot the question, too.

SHARE THE FUN . . .
SHARE YOUR NEW-FOUND TREASURE!!

You don't want to let your new books out of your sight?
That's okay. Your friends can get their own. Order below.

No. 160 SLEIGHT OF HAND by Laura Resnick
Chance and Ally make sparks of the wrong kind—but the show must go on!

No. 161 LUKE'S LADY by Mara Fitzcharles
Luke and Mandy have a "no strings" relationship. What could go wrong?

No. 162 SUMMER'S FORTUNE by Joan Reeves
Summer has a master plan but Ben interferes every step of the way.

No. 163 HIS WOMAN'S GIFT by Lacey Dancer
Eve's love of life touched Sloane and made him think, wish and remember.

No. 164 MINOR ADJUSTMENTS by Beverly Sommers
Anatoly didn't understand Ronnie's rules . . . or he just didn't want to!

No. 165 PARIS WHEN IT SIZZLES by Julie Kistler
Annie was feisty! She was a challenge Trevor just couldn't pass up.

No. 166 BETTING ON LOVE by Ann Patrick
Shawn knew she should steer clear of Michael. He was trouble, for sure.

No. 167 PLAYING LOVE'S ODDS by Michaila Callan
Hannah hires Logan and he's caught in a tangled web of his own making.

Meteor Publishing Corporation
Dept. 893, P. O. Box 41820, Philadelphia, PA 19101-9828

Please send the books I've indicated below. Check or money order (U.S. Dollars only)—no cash, stamps or C.O.D.s (PA residents, add 6% sales tax). I am enclosing $2.95 plus 75¢ handling fee for *each* book ordered.

Total Amount Enclosed: $_____.

___ No. 168	___ No. 150	___ No. 156	___ No. 162
___ No. 145	___ No. 151	___ No. 157	___ No. 163
___ No. 146	___ No. 152	___ No. 158	___ No. 164
___ No. 147	___ No. 153	___ No. 159	___ No. 165
___ No. 148	___ No. 154	___ No. 160	___ No. 166
___ No. 149	___ No. 155	___ No. 161	___ No. 167

Please Print:
Name _____

Address _____ Apt. No. _____

City/State _____ Zip _____

Allow four to six weeks for delivery. Quantities limited.